DEATH AT THE BBC

DEATH
AT THE
BBC

JOHN SHERWOOD

CHARLES SCRIBNER'S SONS
NEW YORK

Library of Congress Cataloging in Publication Data

Sherwood, John.
  Death at the BBC.

  Previously published as: A shot in the arm. 1982.
  I. Title.   II. Title: Death at the B.B.C.
PR6037.H517S5   1983   823'.914   83-9082
ISBN 0-684-17990-3

225297

M
She

AUTHOR'S NOTE

The characters in this book exemplify tendencies and attitudes which were current in and around the BBC in 1937. They are composite figures invented to serve the plot and are not to be identified with anyone working in radio at the time. In particular the central character of the Features Organiser bears no resemblance whatever to the late Laurence Gilliam, who presided with great distinction over features output from 1936 till his death in 1964.

I have, however, followed fact in presenting Sir John Reith, as he then was, as a very remote yet all-pervading presence. During his last months as Director-General he took little part in the day-to-day running of the Corporation.

"I am certain of this, that to set out to give the public what it wants—as the saying is—is a dangerous and fallacious policy, involving almost certainly an underestimate of public intelligence and a continual lowering of standards."

John Reith: Into the Wind

"It was John Reith's ambition . . . to let the outside world see the Corporation as he saw it as the dependable keeper of the nation's conscience. Its rightful position was that of an arbiter standing above the clamour of all political and social factions. As the paragon of impartiality, honesty and respectability, its good name had to be defended at all costs."

Andrew Boyle: Only the Wind will Listen

"With ingenuity and a little luck a creative person can persuade (or fool) some of the administrators some of the time."

Louis MacNeice

"I do not think that any moral objection can attach to letting people know at what price any horse ran."

BBC Internal Memo

PART ONE

*In which those concerned
Praise the Lord
and Pass the Ammunition*

ONE

"WHY CAN'T WE just live apart?"

"Because I've decided to divorce you."

"I'd have to resign. You know the Corporation rule."

"Yes, but the upright and God-fearing BBC should move with the times. This is 1937, not the Middle Ages."

"In other words you propose to create a divorce scandal and wreck my career."

"The sooner it grinds to a halt the better, if it consists of no-pun-intended with your secretary in sleazy provincial hotels."

"The Midland in Manchester isn't sleazy. Anyway we didn't as you very well know."

"I bet you did in Edinburgh to keep warm."

"She wasn't there. Peter Warren took his girl, and we didn't need two."

"Knowing Peter Warren's secretary, I'm not surprised."

"What nonsense, she's well over forty."

"That only makes the whole thing more nauseous."

"Angie, this isn't you talking. It's a disease that's got into your mind. Please be sensible. Go back into the flat and get dressed."

She had pursued him out into the corridor in her pyjamas. The third floor corridor of Imperial Mansions in St John's Wood was no place for this sort of conversation even with both parties fully dressed, and a charwoman was hovering near the lifts with a duster. Tony Chatham tried to shoo his wife back into their flat, but she sidestepped.

"Don't touch me! And don't try soft soap, my heels are firmly dug in."

"Angie, be reasonable—"

"No. Why should I sit there like a ninny, waiting for you to poison me so that you can indulge your nasty urges?"

"My dear Angie, you're imagining things."

"Why was there that sinister stain in my teacup?"

"Because Mrs Marsh hadn't washed it up properly. You say the coffee was bitter. We swapped cups. I drank yours. There was nothing wrong with it. You're ill. *Please* see Dr Fellows."

"I am *not* ill, I'm as healthy as the Statue of Liberty. I shall talk to the lawyer today."

He ran over the arguments again. The British Broadcasting Corporation was still earning its place as a national institution. It had to be trusted in high quarters, therefore it could not afford bohemianism or scandal. If it came to a divorce he would be expected to resign at once. The BBC was his life. If she insisted they could live apart. But divorce, no.

"It's after ten, I must go," he added. "I've a meeting at half past. I'll try to get away early, promise me not to do anything till we've talked again."

She shook her head obstinately. "I shall divorce you, just like that."

She was shouting. The charwoman had stopped pretending not to listen.

"Go and get dressed, for heaven's sake," Chatham muttered, and gave her a push.

"How dare you touch me, you rampant lecher!" she shrieked, and slapped his face hard. Ugly with anger, she ran into the flat and slammed the door.

Tony Chatham made off towards the lift, past the staring charwoman. Having overheard everything, she was surprised that he did not look agitated. More grim and determined-like, with a faraway look in his eyes. One of those regular faces that just missed being offensively handsome. Nice, though.

The determined look on Chatham's face hid sickening tension. His feature programmes on the National Programme were prestige events. They got respectful treatment by the radio critics and to judge from the BBC's mailbag serious listeners liked them. Since his promotion two years ago he had been running the Features Unit. He enjoyed striking sparks out of other people and sometimes got out of them first-class programmes that he could never have put together himself. He had just got things going nicely, with the right amount of tension and a good mix of contrasting talents. All this was threatened, unless . . .

As he waited for the lift he forced himself to pretend that this was a normal day, and glanced down the front page of *The Times*. No one he knew had died or married or given birth, so he opened it and studied the headlines on the bill page inside. Mussolini was in Berlin on a visit to Hitler, they had both addressed a huge crowd in the Olympic Stadium. "Herr Hitler's speech . . ." He had to be called "Herr" Hitler because disrespect might provoke another outburst, and outbursts by Hitler, even if played down discreetly by the press, were bad for business confidence. Something had been cobbled together to save British and French faces over non-intervention in the Spanish Civil War, and someone had flown the Atlantic in ten hours thirty-three minutes, but there seemed to be a lull in bomb outrages in Northern Ireland and Palestine. Roosevelt's speech had come too late for a full report—it would be in tomorrow's *Times*. One day, perhaps, the press barons would relent and let the BBC broadcast news throughout the day. It was ridiculous having the first bulletin after six at night, so that they could sell their papers without competition from radio. . . . He rode down in the lift, trying to shut disquieting thoughts from his mind, but failed miserably.

Imperial Mansions faced on to the north side of Regent's Park. The late September sunshine striking through the autumn trees did nothing to cheer him. He crossed the road and waited for an empty cab to come along. Presently one did, from the direction of the zoo.

Bill Atkinson, the cab driver, was in a bad mood, having been rewarded with a sixpenny tip for depositing a large family party at the zoo gates. He studied his next fare, who stood by the kerb with his arm raised to hail the cab; a tall, fairish man in a fawn overcoat with a velvet collar. A rather set face like an army officer's on a parade ground. But he wore no hat, so could not be a guardee in mufti and anyway his hair was a little too long. Probably a gent, though, when it came to tipping.

Ten yards to go. As Atkinson braked he heard a sharp crack, not quite the sound of a car backfiring. For a moment the tall man stood rigid beside the kerb. Then his upraised arm fell to his side. He clutched it and crumpled into the gutter.

Atkinson jumped from his cab and hurried forward. What with all the talk of war he had been to some first aid classes. He did what he could but knew it was not enough. As people began to run up he got Chatham, bleeding heavily, into the cab and shot off, using all the short cuts and side street dodges he knew, towards the casualty department of the Middlesex Hospital.

TWO

WHEN BROADCASTING HOUSE was new five years earlier, the architectural press had likened it to a stone battleship anchored at the top of Upper Regent Street with its prow pointing down the vista towards Oxford Circus. Once one got past the grand entrance hall and reception desk the narrow, low-ceilinged passages certainly recalled the bowels of a ship. Off the fifth floor corridor near the prow, overlooking the angle of Upper Regent Street and Portland Place, was an office with a card outside the door which read: Mr A. H. Chatham, Features Organiser; Miss D. Rowlandson, Secretary.

But Miss D. Rowlandson, Secretary, was speeding towards Liverpool on a boat train to take passage to Canada where her mother, it appeared, was dangerously ill. Miss Jennifer Howe, typing pool, had been flung into the breach and was doing her best to cope with the telephone of a man she had never seen who had failed to turn up at his office for no known reason.

Jennifer Howe had a creditable honours degree in English, but not from Oxford or Cambridge and therefore inferior in the Corporation's eyes. Despite the rearmament boom jobs were still scarce and she knew she was lucky to have one. At her interview she had been told firmly that if she planned to break through the secretarial barrier and get her hands on a programme post she had better think again. She had no such exaggerated hopes, but was bored by the drudgery of copy-typing scripts and programmes-as-broadcast in the typing pool. Something a little better might come into view if she acquitted herself well as a substitute for the absent Miss Rowlandson.

Some of the telephone queries could be answered by reference to Mr Chatham's well-filled desk trays. Advice could also be had from the nearby office of his deputy, a Mr P. R. Warren, Secretary

Miss L. Mannerton. But Lavinia Mannerton's advice was not always explicit. "Probably in his pending tray," she had murmured, when asked about some urgently needed copy for the *Radio Times*. But Mr Chatham's pending tray was stacked high, and a uniformed messenger from the *Radio Times* stood by unnervingly while she searched. Meanwhile the telephone was ringing, and horrors, it was not an ordinary call. The switchboard had given the dreaded three rings.

Hoping it might be a mistake she waited and let the girl on the board repeat the performance. But there was no error, so she unhooked the receiver from the solidly built iron daffodil of a telephone and said: "Mr Chatham's office."

There was a pause, as if to mark astonishment and shock. "Who *is* that?" cried a harsh female voice.

"I'm a relief from General Office. Mr Chatham's secretary isn't here."

"I see. But what is your *name*?"

Jennifer told her.

"But surely, Miss Howe, they explained to you on your training course that when the switchboard gives three rings *the call is from the Director-General's office and should be left for Mr Chatham to answer in person on the extension.*"

"But Mr Chatham isn't here. He isn't in the building," Jennifer objected.

"Then where is he?"

"No one seems to know. I rang his home, but—"

"Today's Thursday. He has his weekly meeting this morning, in preparation for the Programme Board this afternoon."

"Yes. They all came and waited for a bit. Then they went back to their offices till he turns up."

"Why isn't Mr Warren deputising for him?"

"Mr Warren isn't here either, not yet. I understand he said he'd be in late."

This confession was not greeted as censoriously as Jennifer expected.

"Oh. One moment . . . Yes, we know where Mr Warren is, that's quite in order. Have you informed Features Executive?"

"About Mr Chatham not being here? Not yet, I've been rather busy."

"But that is the first thing you should have done, Miss Howe. The Executives exist alongside the creative departments of the Corporation to relieve them of administrative routine and help with emergencies such as this. I suggest that you ring Features Executive at once."

"I will as soon as I can, but there's a messenger here waiting for some copy for the *Radio Times*."

"Oh really, I'd better ring them myself. And please tell Mr Chatham, when he appears, that the Director-General would like a word with him on the telephone."

Jennifer added this to her list of messages and went on searching through the pending tray.

"Hullo dear, are you surviving?" asked Lavinia Mannerton's throaty voice from the doorway. She was an elegantly thin woman in an elderly but expensive suit covered with cigarette ash. Her hair was cut short in an Eton crop. Her face would soon cease to have a ravaged beauty and become merely ravaged, and her *l'Aimant de Coty* warred with the smell of her cigarette ash.

Jennifer was still searching. "There's nothing here that looks like a programme billing for the *Radio Times*."

"Oh my dear, I'm covered with shame, didn't I say? It's a feature article, not a billing. Telling the great British public how lucky they are to have such a wonderful Features Unit in their wonderful BBC."

Wishing she had been told this before, Jennifer pulled something out of the pile. "I think this must be it."

It did indeed appear from the two typewritten pages that Features Unit consisted of uniquely gifted beings engaged in flawless, dedicated activity in an atmosphere of mutual admiration.

"Goodness," said Jennifer.

"Auto-erotic is the word you want, dear," said Lavinia languidly. "The Corporation loves sucking its collective thumb."

Jennifer despatched the messenger, with apologies for keeping him waiting.

"Can I solve any other mysteries?" Lavinia asked.

"No, I'm managing, thanks. And someone called Features Executive is being sent to help me cope."

"A fat lot of help that will be. Who made this unfortunate arrangement?"

"A haughty lady in DG's office, who rang to say he wants to talk to Mr Chatham. Why, is Features Executive not a helpful person?"

"Oh, he won't come himself, dear. He'll send his horrid minion to create chaos out of order. How vexing, we don't want old mother Prodnose snuffling around down here."

"If Mr Chatham turns up we can send her away," said Jennifer.

"True, but where *is* Tony? Ring his home number again."

Jennifer hesitated. "When I rang before, Mrs Chatham sounded rather . . . odd."

"Ah, but if Angela was stinkers at half past ten she'll be horizontal in a stupor by now. With any luck the daily help will answer and we'll get some sense."

Jennifer rang but there was no reply. She looked ruefully at her lengthening list of urgent telephone messages. "Perhaps Mr Warren can help with some of these when he gets here. Where is he, though? The DG's haughty lady was very mysterious about it."

"Simple, dear, but oh *hush*. He's at Buck House."

Thanks to a schoolfriend with a brother in the Brigade of Guards, Jennifer recognised this allusion to the Palace.

"Why is it such a secret?"

"All dealings with Buck House have to be stealthy, dear, by official BBC decree. They're afraid if it's talked about people who go there will get uppish and people who don't will get jealous, I can't think why. When I was a sweet young debutante my mother dragged me there in feathers and a train and the chandeliers made everyone look green except Queen Mary who looked like a wax-work of herself and it was a frightful bore."

"But what is Mr Warren doing at the Palace?"

"That's even more oh hush. He's grappling with the royal impediment problem. Because, you see, he's in charge of the Christmas Day hook-up."

Jennifer did see. The Christmas Day broadcast to the nation and Empire was a revered BBC institution and a brilliant technical display of the resources of that miracle of modern science, the wireless. Messages of goodwill flowed in to Broadcasting House over radio and undersea cable circuits from every corner of the world that was coloured red on the map. As they came in they were broadcast, live, for British subjects everywhere to hear. Cathedral choirs, the bells of Bethlehem and dialect-speaking shepherds from the Lake District were thrown in for good measure, building up to the climax at three o'clock, when the countless millions of the Empire heard the homely, reassuring tones of their sovereign, King George the Fifth, delivering his Christmas message to them from Sandringham.

But George the Fifth had been dead for well over a year.

"It really was very naughty of Edward the Abdicator," said Lavinia, "vanishing with his fancy lady and landing brother George with this job. Just imagine the countless millions of the Empire listening to the struggles of a monarch with lots of impediment and hardly any speech."

"But can't they record him and edit it?"

"Oh no, dear, that's what's known as Breaking Faith with the Public. However—" She broke off, and said languidly, "Oh hullo, Miss Proctor. Good news, Jennifer, salvation is at hand, here's Features Executive to the rescue."

"I think I heard the telephone ring in your office, Miss Mannerton," said the newcomer tartly.

"You didn't Miss Proctor, dear, because I was listening. But if you're casting aspersions I'd better go."

Jennifer decided that Miss Proctor, *alias* old mother Prodnose, had taken far too literally the cosmetics advertisers' message that ugly women could enjoy sexual prosperity provided they were impeccably groomed. Miss Proctor was ruthlessly primped and curled and had applied dabs of hectic colour to her face, having been encouraged by the beauty writers to believe that these, if strategically placed, would distract the observer's attention from her enormous nose.

"Now let's start sorting out your troubles, Miss Howe," she

began. "I'm sorry you're overwhelmed, it's not your fault. They should never have sent you here."

"I don't think I'm overwhelmed."

"But DG's secretary says you are."

"Well, she's obviously a lady who knows her own mind," said Jennifer, realising too late that this was a subversive remark.

Miss Proctor sniffed, and picked up Jennifer's typewritten sheet of messages.

"Who is this Mr Olivier who queried his fee?"

"He's an actor. He says television's paying him barely half what he got for playing Cromwell in that radio feature of Mr Chatham's."

"Ridiculous. Radio has a mass following of millions. Television's just a gimmick for a tiny audience of rich people in the London area, of course the Corporation doesn't pay the same fees. What did you tell him?"

"I said I'd give Mr Chatham the message, but perhaps he'd like to take it up direct with Television Service at Alexandra Palace."

Miss Proctor sniffed again, but offered no verbal criticism. Before she could find fault with anything else the door crashed open to admit a heavily built man with a large pale face and untidy yellow curls and a lot of shirt tail showing between the waistcoat and trousers of an otherwise formal suit.

"Who the hell are you?" he asked, staring at Jennifer. "You look rather nice."

"Miss Howe is from the pool," said Miss Proctor, making her sound like the lowest form of pond life.

He rounded on her. "How now, Miss Proctor you secret black and midnight hag, what is't you do?"

Seeing that quotations from Macbeth were in order, Jennifer refrained with difficulty from asking, "What bloody man is that?"

"Oh really, Mr Warren, there's no need to be offensive," protested the painted lady.

He rounded on her. "Go away, Miss Proctor. Hence horrible shadow, unreal mockery hence. Let me enjoy Miss Howe."

"I shall do nothing of the kind, Mr Warren. Miss Howe has been

sent up from the pool and everything is in chaos. I am sorting it
out."

"With ruin upon ruin, rout on rout, confusion worse con-
founded," said Warren, switching to Milton. "Where's Tony?"

"Nobody knows where Mr Chatham is," said Miss Proctor in
public-prosecutor tones.

"Pity. I've come to gloat. He tried to blue-pencil one of my
features, but I've got DG to overrule him, it's quite easy if you
know how to handle DG."

"This is no concern of ours, Mr Warren," said Miss Proctor.

"It's everyone's concern, too much gets swept under the carpet
in this place. Why shouldn't the miners broadcast about what
Conservative economic policy's doing to them?"

"Miss Howe and I are busy, Mr Warren. Please leave us alone."

"Okay, but let me know when he comes in." In the doorway he
turned and gave Jennifer a pleasantly mischievous wink.

He went. Miss Proctor's face was a study in lewd venom. "You
need to watch him," she hissed obscenely. "His shirt isn't the only
thing he can't keep inside his trousers."

It was almost lunch time before she pronounced herself satisfied
and rose. "I'll try to get someone more experienced in here
tomorrow, Miss Howe, and you can go back to the pool."

Jennifer ate her lunch, consisting of an apple and a piece of
cheese, on a bench in the autumn sun of Regent's Park. When she
got back to the office a tall, rather handsome man sat slumped
behind the desk by the window. His face was drained of all colour
and his arm was in a sling.

"Are you Mr Chatham?"

He made an effort to concentrate. "Yes. You must be . . . the
relief secretary. What's your name?"

Jennifer told him and added: "Everyone's been worried. Has
there been an accident?"

"Oh . . . Yes, didn't the hospital phone through a message?"

"No, Mr Chatham."

"I asked them to . . ." He picked up her typewritten sheet of
notes. "You seem to have coped very sensibly, Jennifer."

"Thank you, Mr Chatham."

"You call me Tony, by the way . . ."

He had manners. There was no coarseness about him. There would be no hot-handed fumbling among the desks, even when his arm was out of the sling.

"I tried to phone DG," he went on, "but he's not back from lunch yet. Let's polish off what we can of this before I have to go down to Programme Board."

For twenty minutes he dictated rapidly but without fuss. As he rose wincing with pain to go to the meeting, the telephone rang. Chatham paused in the doorway. But the switchboard gave only one ring.

"It's not DG," he said. "I'm not here."

"It's Reception," she reported. "Mrs Chatham is in the entrance hall asking for you."

Chatham's face became even greyer and more desperate. "I must attend this meeting."

"But you're not well. Shouldn't you let Mr Warren deputise and go home with Mrs Chatham?"

"I can't do that," he said sharply. "Jennifer, this is a frightful thing to ask, but you seem very sensible and nice and . . . my wife isn't well, you see, I think she's having a sort of nervous breakdown. When she's told I'm in a meeting and can't see her she may . . . make a disturbance in the entrance hall. Would you mind awfully going down and trying to keep her as quiet as possible?"

"Of course. I'll do my best."

"Bless you. Try to persuade her to go home, or—look, here's some money, if necessary take her home yourself in a cab. And don't discuss my . . . accident with her, it would only upset her more."

"Very well, Mr—Tony. Wait, you're forgetting your papers for the meeting."

Chatham took them. With his wound throbbing and his head dizzy, he started down the corridor. By the lift he almost collided with someone.

"Tony! What on earth's happened?"

It was Helen Thackeray. No one else was in earshot. She was one of the few colleagues he could trust.

"You look awful," she said. "What have you done to your arm?"

"Angela tried to shoot me," said Chatham.

The lift arrived, crowded with staff on the way to the Council Chamber for the meeting.

"Come to my room afterwards," murmured Helen, stepping in. "Then we can talk."

THREE

THE ENTRANCE HALL at Broadcasting House had already started to look outdated, though several decades were to pass before it became a carefully preserved example of the"modernistic"taste of the early thirties.

"She's over there in the Chanel suit," said the receptionist in answer to Jennifer's enquiry.

A dark-haired woman, impeccably casual in grey flannel, stood in the middle of the floor, twisting her gloves and ignoring the bustle about her.

Jennifer approached her nervously. "Mrs Chatham? I'm afraid your husband's in a meeting. Can I help at all?"

Angela Chatham studied her with mad-looking pale grey eyes. "That depends on who you are."

"I'm standing in for his secretary. She's away."

"Ah yes. She's about to produce what's vulgarly known as a 'little stranger', so he shipped her off to Canada. Don't let him do that to you, he's very careless."

"There's no question of it, Mrs Chatham."

"Don't you be too sure. My husband's a teapot. When he sees teacups he fills them."

"Not if the teacups are turned upside down," said Jennifer.

Mrs Chatham gave a mad little giggle. "You're fun, I like you. But do watch him, he's keen on quiet girls like you with good clear skins. You see, he's wicked. He's been trying to poison me, there was a funny mark inside my teacup and my coffee tasted bitter."

"I'm sure you must be mistaken, he was very concerned for you."

It was as if she had administered an electric shock. "Why, you silly little tart, how dare you?" Mrs Chatham shouted. "He's turned you against me already."

People had turned to stare, but fortunately there was a diversion. The two commissionaires at the entrance doors snapped to attention. A third shooed everyone out of a crowded lift which was about to start its upward journey and stood inside it waiting. And into the hall, with its inscription in Latin which included his own name, strode the immensely tall eagle-browed figure of the Director-General.

The onlookers seemed to stop breathing. Reith, the founding father of the BBC, had become a legend in his lifetime. He had fought the politicians and the press barons and the vested interests of the radio industry and created a national institution. He had said proudly that he did not care how much of the weekend audience was lost to commercial stations on the continent, while he was Director-General the BBC would not broadcast jazz on Sundays. Lately his passage through the entrance hall had caused ripples of apprehension as well as awe. There had been rumours for months that he was about to move on to a high Government post. Changes were overdue, everyone knew that. But Reith *was* the BBC. It was frightening to think of it without his firm grip, sailing on (under whose direction?) into the unknown.

As Reith strode on towards the open lift Mrs Chatham called, "Sir John, one moment please," in an imperious society-hostess voice.

"Please, Mrs Chatham," Jennifer begged, "don't make a scene."

"Nonsense, I must warn him about Tony."

Everyone stared at the creator of this unheard-of disturbance except Sir John Reith, who strode on looking neither to left nor right till the lift doors closed behind him.

"This place is full of hypocrites," Mrs Chatham shouted.

"Mrs Chatham, *please*. I expect you'd like to leave a message for your husband, come and sit over here and tell me what to say."

"Yes, what a good idea." She gave Jennifer a rather mad smile. "Tell him I'm going down to Fontbury tonight on the late train, and he's not to follow me. If he does I shall walk down the village street telling everyone at the top of my voice about that disgusting orgy of his with the girl guides among the rhododendrons. Well?

Don't stand there staring, you silly cow, I'm going home. Tell the commissionaire to get me a cab."

"She must have smuggled one of the guns up from Fontbury in her luggage," said Chatham. "Luckily she only got me in the arm."

"You ought to go home and rest," Helen Thackeray suggested.

"I'm all right . . ." But he did not look it.

The meeting was over and he had made straight for Helen's office. She was a generation older than him and he had started his BBC career as one of her talented young men. He still treated her as his mother confessor. She had straight hair worn in a bun, no make-up and a first class brain which had won her a key post high up on the programme side; so high that she was entitled to an armchair in her office.

"Angela's serious about the divorce," said Chatham, leaning back wearily in the armchair. "In so far as a person having a nervous breakdown can be serious about anything."

"We can't let her wreck your career," said Helen.

"What's there to stop her? She's insanely jealous and now I've inherited Fontbury she can come down on me for a lot of alimony."

Fontbury was an exquisite little manor house in Berkshire. A substantial income went with it.

"I'm astonished, Tony. You seemed so happy together."

"Yes, it only started two months ago. She'd been very moody, I'd noticed that. What I hadn't grasped was she'd decided for no reason at all that I was having an affair with Daphne Rowland-son."

"That blonde secretary of yours?"

"Yes, but I was no more interested in her than I imagine she was in me, and in my innocence I took her up to Manchester with me when I went there to sort out that muddle about the Joseph Arkwright feature. We stayed at the Midland and Daphne was in and out of my bedroom at all hours with rush typing jobs and it turned out that Angela had hired a private enquiry agent to observe these comings and goings. When she got his report she made a frightful scene and the whole thing came out into the open."

26

"But surely," Helen objected, "the detective has to swear in court that he saw the guilty party and the co-respondent in bed together."

"The court's often satisfied if it's proved that the couple spent long enough shut up in a bedroom for adultery to be presumed." Chatham hesitated. "I dictated to Daphne quite a lot late at night."

"What sort of impression would Miss Rowlandson make in the witness box?"

"She won't be there. Angela went to her home and called her a whore and a lot of other beastly things in front of her parents. Daphne decided in everyone's interest to clear out, she has family in Canada. I helped her with her passage."

"Dear me, what an uncomfortable kettle of fish," Helen murmured. He had told her the truth, she was sure of that. Though cheerfully virginal herself she was worldly-wise enough to spot those of her male colleagues who were liable to behave like oversexed goats, and could tell them at a glance from the sexually fastidious sheep. An intrigue with a secretary was not Chatham's style.

"The ban on divorces isn't quite as rigid as it was," said Chatham hopefully. "He has made exceptions."

"Mostly for people in Variety Department or Television. They don't matter, he expects them to behave like animals. We're different."

"Then you don't think I've got a chance?"

Helen thought. Nowadays each case was supposed to be considered on its merits, but publicised adultery between two members of staff was still unforgivable.

"If only it wasn't your secretary," she said. "Can't you arrange with Angela not to cite her?"

"No, I've tried that. She *wants* to wreck my career. If it comes to court I shan't fight it, I shall resign."

"Oh no, that mustn't happen," said Helen, trying to control the trembling of her voice. She was deeply distressed for him. She had singled him out before he had been in the Corporation a month, seen his potential, moved him round to make sure he got the right experience. Drama Department had never forgiven her for carving out of it a separate Features Unit for him to be head of, and she still had to defend him against the drama pundits' claws at every Programme Board. She had intended the Features job as a stepping stone to higher management, but now all that was threatened.

"If you leave they'll put Peter Warren into your job," she lamented. "He'll be a disaster, wrecking everything and jeering at all the broadcasting techniques we've pioneered."

"I know Peter upsets people. But he has some good ideas."

"My dear Tony, he broadcasts *unscripted discussions*. Chaos! People just aren't capable of expressing themselves coherently at the microphone without a script, everyone knows that. There'd be nothing on the air but 'off' voices and unscripted drivel."

Chatham agreed with Warren that the airwaves could not be monopolised forever by superior-sounding speakers of standard English reading from scripts, and supported his attempts to move with the times. But he let that pass.

"They'd put someone in over him," he objected.

"Don't you believe it. He's ambitious and he knows how to curry favour at the top. Going round saying speakers are over-exposed and so on."

The top brass, fearful of the power of broadcasters who became too popular, was happy to listen to such suggestions and banish the over-successful from the air.

"He was wrong about John Hilton," Chatham admitted.

John Hilton was a commentator with a large popular following. Back in the summer Warren had started proclaiming that Hilton was "stale". In July the management took Hilton off the air, on the ground that he was "in danger of being ruined by excessive publicity and success", and Warren was triumphant.

"That was a special case," Helen murmured. She could not tell Chatham the real story, which was a management secret. One of her predecessors had observed that "an impression of left wing bias is always liable to be created by a speaker who voices unfamiliar views". Hilton, a victim of this sad truth, had been taken off the air under Government pressure.

"Peter often suggests new speakers who are brilliant successes," Chatham argued.

"Exactly, he's attracting the attention of all the people who'll take the decisions when Reith goes, it's only a matter of time. He even managed to get the Christmas broadcast away from you."

"I asked him to take it over for a change."

"Only after he'd told everyone it was getting into a rut. And look what happened this afternoon."

Chatham had just been publicly overruled at the Programme Board in a disagreement with his deputy. Warren wanted to include some caustic remarks by Welsh miners about Conservative government policy in a feature which was supposed to be about the music of the Welsh valleys. Chatham had told him to cut it. There was an unspoken temporary taboo on such vexing matters for fear of upsetting some delicate negotiations with a Whitehall committee. But Warren had appealed to the DG, who had overruled Chatham. The ruling, delivered at the meeting, had been accompanied by a lecture on the need to be flexible and judge each case on its merits.

"DG might have warned you first," said Helen.

"He tried to phone, but I was at the hospital having lead extracted from my arm. There are these rumours. Is he really moving on? How soon?"

"Goodness knows. He's been offered Imperial Airways, but I think he's hanging on in the hope of something better."

"If he goes soon I might not have to resign. The next DG may be more reasonable over divorce."

"Less firm in his principles," Helen corrected. "But I hope you're right."

"Mrs Chatham?"

She had vaguely noticed the two men, waiting at the entrance of Imperial Mansions as she paid off the cab. They had given her two minutes to take off her hat and gloves, then followed her up to the flat and rung the bell.

"Detective-Sergeant Verney, Metropolitan Police," said the pink faced fuzzy-haired one, proffering a card. "And this is my assistant, Detective-Constable Burton."

"Yes?" said Mrs Chatham.

"It's about the incident this morning in which your husband was involved."

"My husband? What incident?"

"Perhaps if I might come inside . . ."

Detective-Constable Burton followed his chief inside and sat looking uncomfortable in a flowery chintz armchair. He did not feel uncomfortable, but he knew that under the class system it was expected of him. While Verney dealt with Mrs Chatham's exclamations of innocent surprise and dismay, Burton's eyes worked their way round the room noting the places where a largish gun could be concealed. According to the staff of Imperial Mansions she was on bad terms with her husband. The windows looked out at the front of the block towards the trees of Regent's Park. Chatham, standing facing the building from across the road, had been shot from in front.

Meanwhile Detective-Sergeant Verney was fawning indecently on the handsome Mrs Chatham in his la-di-da public school accent, and Mrs Chatham was congratulating herself on having to deal with a nice young man from Lord Trenchard's new Police College at Hendon, and not with a member of the lower orders. No, she had no idea that her husband had been shot at, nor who could have done such a thing. Soon after he left the building? She had heard nothing, she must have been in her bath. No, she had not been in touch with her husband during the day, except—yes, she had called at Broadcasting House for a word with him, but he had refused to see her.

"I ought to explain," she added, "that we're getting divorced."

"I have to ask as a formality," said Verney, "do you possess a firearm of any kind?"

"Yes," she said, smiling. "You'll find it next door, in the drawer on the right-hand side of the bed."

Burton made no move. Verney shot him a look, and went to fetch it himself. Mrs Chatham gave Burton a condescending smile. "Our house in Berkshire is rather isolated. I have a licence for the gun, of course."

Verney came back with a dainty little revolver, which would be inaccurate at twenty feet and harmless at twenty yards. It was loaded, but showed no sign of having been fired.

"As a matter of routine," said Verney, "would you mind if Constable Burton and I had a look round? In your own interest, I'd like to satisfy myself that there isn't a weapon of the kind we're looking for concealed anywhere in the flat."

"Oh do, please," said Mrs Chatham, lolling back among the cushions and lighting a cigarette.

They began searching. Burton pointed out coldly that Verney had overlooked the broom cupboard in the passage, then flipped open the dirty linen basket in the bathroom.

"That's too small to hide a gun in," said Verney.

Without comment, Burton drew out a bloodstained shirt.

"Oh," said Verney.

"Came home from the hospital to change, then went on to the office," Burton remarked.

They went into the bedroom. Burton gave himself the pleasure of pointing out to his embarrassed superior several obvious hiding places that he had overlooked. He was a firm supporter of the Police Federation, which was waging a fierce battle against Lord Trenchard's new Police College, and Verney was one of its first graduates. The college existed to train men already in the force, but Trenchard had rashly arranged direct entry for a few recruits of superior educational background and according to the Police Federation this was a plot to impose on the Metropolitan Police a public-school officer class of chinless Lord Peter Wimseys without the brains. Constable Burton, twenty years in the force and underpaid, was doing everything he could to lower Verney's morale and see that this case did him no credit.

"Well? What shall we do next?" Verney asked uncertainly.

"Whatever you say, sarge."

"If she shot him, she's had hours to get rid of the gun. Let's see if the husband can give us a lead, we can phone him from Vine Street."

Burton made no comment. He had taken the hall porter aside and asked a question which Verney ought to have had the sense to

31

put. When Mrs Chatham left Imperial Mansions that morning, she had been carrying only a small handbag. Perhaps the weapon had not left the building, they ought to search it from top to bottom. But if Verney wanted to go back to Vine Street, well and good. At least it would mean a sit-down and a cup of tea, and while they were drinking it he would point out Verney's mistake to him and watch him squirm.

FOUR

"HE'S BACK IN his office now," said Lavinia Mannerton.

Peter Warren heaved himself up clumsily from behind his desk. "About bloody time too, the meeting broke up hours ago. I shall now go in there and rub the grapes of my stored-up wrath all over his silly cowpat of a face."

"If you want to seduce that new girl he's got in there," said Lavinia, filing her nails, "you'd better watch your language. She looks to me the vicar's daughter type."

Warren shot her a look of pure hatred, then ambled off round the curve of the corridor towards Chatham's office and threw open the door so hard that it crashed against the filing cabinet and made Jennifer wince. His appearance had deteriorated still further since the morning. The formal suit which had passed muster at Buckingham Palace was now covered with cigarette ash. The waistcoat, collar and tie were undone and his belly, plus a good deal of shirt, was escaping from his trouser band. He plumped himself down on a corner of Jennifer's desk with his back to her.

"So the DG overruled you, Tony," he began, "and my Welsh miners are to have their say after all."

"Yes," said Chatham, with his eyes shut.

"This is what happens when an autocracy falls into decay, Tony old man. Reith sits there at the top like a mad old dreamer of a Tsar, and all the eager courtiers like you try to curry favour and pander to his manias. 'He doesn't like this so we'll blue-pencil it, but he loves that so we'll bore the listeners' pants off with it.' Then one day the arse-creeping courtiers find out that he's quite sane and doesn't have any manias, and he sacks the lot of them for making him and the BBC look bloody silly. Hurt your arm, have you?"

"Yes," said Chatham. "I'm rather busy, what can I do for you?"

33

"You can stop weaving mischief and undo your latest knavish trick."

Chatham opened one eye. "Do please explain."

"You know the Vasco da Gama feature. It's intricate. I'm using five studios. There's a lot of music."

"So you told me."

"And I'm using the Theatre Orchestra."

"You told me that too."

"And some filthy sneak has tipped off Music Executive. They say we've got to use their balance and control team instead of ours. Hell, using a strange team will wreck the feature, you know that, it's what you wanted, Tony, isn't it? . . . No, don't pretend to look surprised, I know damn well who sneaked, it was you."

Chatham sat up like a comically startled owl. "Don't be absurd, Peter. Of course I didn't."

But Warren repeated his accusation, working himself up into a fury but keeping a wary eye on Chatham as if playing some kind of game. He reminded Jennifer of an over-excited child seeing how far it could go before its father lost his temper and hit it.

As he ranted, Chatham rose to his full height, wincing with pain from his arm. "Shut up, Peter, and listen to me. Your bad manners and your prima donna airs have made every producer in this unit hate your guts. I wouldn't be surprised if they'd all rung Features Executive one after the other. I'll do what I can, but if you have to produce with a strange balance and control team you'll have only yourself to thank. Now get out of here, and stay out till you're sent for."

"I'll go when you've rung someone senior enough to stop this nonsense," Warren shouted, lunging forward and confronting him across the desk. Suddenly they were both yelling at once. Jennifer, who had been trying for some time to vanish tactfully, managed to squeeze past and escape to Warren's office, where Lavinia sat painting her nails.

"I imagine I'm not wanted when that sort of thing happens," said Jennifer.

"It's safer to be elsewhere, dear, if two men start fighting in a room that size. About the Vasco da Gama feature, was it?"

34

"Yes, something about Music Executive and the Theatre Orchestra. I didn't understand."

"I'll let you into a secret, dear. There are two BBCs. One of them exists in DG's mind and in a mass of written rules and regulations. The other BBC is what really happens, because the rules and regulations are unworkable. But Music Executive and Features Executive and all the other executives spend their time trying to find out what the creative departments are up to and telling them to stop it because it's against the rules."

"I see," said Jennifer. "It sounded as if Music Executive had caught us out doing something quite illegal."

"They have, dear. You see, Features Unit has its own balance and control team that Peter and Tony are used to working with—"

"They're the people who place the microphones and man the control panel and so on?"

"Yes. But the regulations say that if you're using an orchestra you have to use Music Department's balance and control staff, who are hopeless at anything except music and drive everyone mad by fussing about the harmonics of the piccolo and to hell with the feature. If everyone keeps quiet we usually get away with using our own team, but this time someone's sneaked."

"Could it have been Mr Chatham?"

Lavinia pondered. "Well, he and Peter have been snapping at each other's ankles lately, but—no, it's not his style, he's too grand for that sort of thing. How d'you get on with him?"

"I like him a lot."

"Careful, don't get any Girls' Own Paper ideas about him, there's nothing in that nonsense of his wife's about a roll in the hay with Daphne Rowlandson. I doubt if he even knows that she fornicated on alternate Thursdays with a married dentist from Balham."

The door crashed open and Warren barged in crossly. "I've told him I'll murder him if he doesn't get this damn nonsense reversed. Sorry, my dear, did my tantrums frighten you?" The smile he threw Jennifer was charming but he spoilt it by putting a warm hand on the shoulder of her thin blouse. "You can go back to your office now, it's all over."

As she left, the other two exchanged an oddly expressive look. Wondering what it meant, she half opened Chatham's door, then paused. He was on the telephone.

"Nonsense, Miss Proctor, she's very efficient and sensible, hasn't put a foot wrong all day . . . Oh, to hell with seniority, I'm not having one of your hennaed battleaxes in here ordering me about. She's staying here till we make a permanent appointment, that's flat."

Closing the door again silently from outside, Jennifer allowed a decent interval to pass, then walked in.

"Ah, good," said Chatham. "I've arranged to keep you here for the present, I hope that's all right?"

"Perfectly, Mr Chatham."

" 'Tony', not 'Mr Chatham'! You've managed very well—and thank you for dealing so tactfully with my wife. I imagine she talked a lot about our personal affairs?"

"Oh, but I realise she wasn't herself, and didn't really mean it. I won't tell anyone."

"Bless you. Sorry it's been a bit hectic."

"I prefer it to the satanic mill of the typing pool," she said, then regretted the hackneyed quotation from Blake.

"I bet it is satanic too. Let's tidy up the loose ends and go home."

While they were doing this the telephone rang. "A Mr Verney," said Jennifer. "He rang while you were in the meeting, but wouldn't state his business."

Chatham picked up the extension.

"Detective-Sergeant Verney here, Vine Street Police Station. It's concerning the incident this morning. We had a report from the Middlesex Hospital."

"Oh yes," said Chatham cautiously with one eye on Jennifer.

"The hospital passed on your message. We appreciate that in view of your position you would prefer to avoid publicity. But of course they had to report a case of wounding with a firearm, so I wondered if it would be convenient for you to call in here on your way home and make a statement?"

"I could manage that," said Chatham. "I'll come round now."

A cab deposited him at the corner of Swallow Street and Vine

Street, just off Piccadilly. He walked up the dead-end of Vine Street and into the police station. It was still early in the evening. A sad-looking whore and two advanced cases of drunk-and-disorderly were the only people in the charge room. Chatham was taken along a carbolic-smelling passage and into a small office where a pink-faced young Detective-Sergeant called Verney who had escaped from the middle classes asked him questions while a fattish proletarian constable called Burton took notes with a permanent expression of disgust on his face. From the look of things he and Verney loathed each other.

Verney was convinced that Angela was the culprit and Chatham made no attempt to persuade him otherwise. "As you probably know, my wife and I are arranging to separate."

"Mrs Chatham spoke of a divorce," said Verney.

"She wants one, but I'm trying to talk her out of it. Under the BBC rules about divorces I'd have to resign, and I've an interesting job there that I rather enjoy."

Detective-Constable Burton drew attention to himself with an ominous throat-clearing noise.

"Yes?" asked Verney crossly.

"I was just thinking, sergeant. It would be logical in the circumstances for Mr Chatham to shoot Mrs Chatham, not vice versa."

Verney looked daggers at him. Evidently they had disagreed violently about whether or not Angela was guilty.

"Concerning the weapon," Verney went on. "Did Mrs Chatham have access to any firearms other than the small revolver she showed us?"

"I'm not sure . . . Or rather, let me be frank about this, sergeant. My wife's in a very nervous state, she may have done something silly. But she's done no real harm. I certainly shan't bring a charge and I hope you won't. It would only make it more difficult for me to persuade her not to start divorce proceedings."

"I appreciate that, Mr Chatham. No doubt my superiors will take it into account when deciding what action to take on my report. But about the weapon, now?"

"We have a country home in Berkshire. The gunroom is kept

locked but of course she knows where the key is kept. It would be quite possible, I'm afraid, for her to help herself to a shotgun."

"No doubt this gunroom contains the usual sporting guns, sir, but how about rifles?"

"A rook rifle. Two, I seem to remember."

"No, sir. We're looking for a weapon of much larger calibre."

Chatham looked bewildered. "Oh—why?"

"Didn't the hospital tell you, sir? It wasn't a shotgun wound. We haven't recovered the bullet, it's probably in the grass on the edge of Regent's Park. But they insist that you were shot with something like a .303 rifle."

"So we were wondering," Burton broke in smugly, "where your wife could have obtained such a weapon."

"She couldn't, as far as I know. Good Lord, this alters everything, I had no idea. The hospital may have told me, but I was groggy after the anaesthetic and didn't take it in."

"So it's possible that your wife wasn't the culprit," said Burton with an I-told-you-so look at Verney.

"And equally possible," said Verney crossly, "that she got hold of a rifle from some source unknown."

"Is she a practised shot with a rifle?" asked Burton.

"I don't know that she's ever fired one. She's quite good with a shotgun, though."

"If I might make a suggestion, sergeant," said Burton sweetly, "we ought to ask Mr Chatham if he has any personal enemies. Apart from his wife."

"Not that I know of. I have professional disagreements with colleagues, of course, but not the sort that ends in a gun battle."

"Or it could be mistaken identity, sergeant," said Burton helpfully. "There's the Palestine question, that's led to a lot of violence lately. Some of the . . . residents in St John's Wood might be affected by that."

Curious, Chatham thought. Because of what was happening in Germany people had instinctively started avoiding the word "Jew".

By the time his statement had been drawn up and signed it was after eight at night. He walked round the corner into Swallow

Street and hailed a cab. As it turned into Piccadilly to head north towards Imperial Mansions a large American car blocked it in for a moment. There was a sharp crack and a tinkle of glass, and the other car surged away into the traffic.

"Crikey, guv, what was that?" asked the cabby.

"I seem to have been shot at," said Chatham, picking glass from the window off his clothes.

The cab jerked to a halt at the kerb and the driver turned to look. "You badly hurt?"

"No. They missed this time, but I'll have to go back to Vine Street. You'd better come in with me . . ."

Back at the police station he marched up to the desk. "I've just been shot at again—get Sergeant Verney. And please, may I use your telephone?"

He rang Imperial Mansions. "Angela? Good, you're still there. I've been shot at."

"So the police tell me, and I don't wonder. You'll have to start seducing your secretaries in a bullet-proof vest."

"Shut up, Angie, and listen. It's just happened again, round the corner in Piccadilly. And the police think it's you taking pot shots at me."

"Not guilty. Though I admit I've been tempted."

"I wish I knew who—Oh, here's Sergeant Verney, I'll put him on. Explain to him how you got from Vine Street to St John's Wood in two minutes flat."

FIVE

THE FIRST HINT at the identity of Chatham's attacker came from Miss Vivienne Brown, a clerk in the Programme Correspondence Unit at Broadcasting House. The unit existed because the BBC did not believe in letting the programme staff receive listeners' letters addressed to them. Praise might go to their heads and they might answer letters of complaint tactlessly or not at all. Their mail was therefore intercepted in Post Room and diverted to PCU for suitable action.

The unit was also supposed to satisfy the curiosity of the programme staff about listener reaction to their broadcasts. The BBC saw no need for systematic audience research. Statistical enquiries would merely confirm what it knew already, namely that what the mass audience really enjoyed was low comedians and cinema organs, whereas the programme policy was to provide more uplifting fare and encourage listeners to acquire a taste for it. But as a sop to the curiosity of the programme departments PCU was given the job of analysing the ramblings of listeners who were sufficiently angry, eccentric or underemployed to write to the BBC. The result of these investigations was presented to all concerned in a weekly report.

Vivienne Brown was examining a file of such correspondence concerning a recent feature about Oliver Cromwell. All she needed was a few representative quotes to make a paragraph in the report. The very long letter she had just picked up, consisting of four closely typewritten foolscap pages, did not look very relevant. She glanced through it and was about to classify it as "unfavourable, incoherent" and put it aside when something about it made her pause.

Vivienne Brown believed that only total disarmament could prevent another world war; and also that the British and French governments ought to put a stop, if necessary by force, to the armed support which Hitler and Mussolini were giving to Franco and his Fascists in the Spanish Civil War. She was therefore a reader of the *Manchester Guardian*, which she devoured anxiously on her way to work instead of reading a novel. It lay at her elbow now, and she remembered a paragraph . . . yes, here it was. On the previous day Mr Anthony Chatham, the well-known BBC producer, had been shot at twice in the street by an unknown assailant.

And the long, very angry letter in her hand was addressed to Anthony Chatham.

After the opening salvo of abuse it launched into a potted history of Ireland, or rather a list of all the grievances of the Irish nation against the English since the beginning of time. Halfway down the last page Miss Brown discovered why Chatham's feature had upset the letter-writer. In a sequence dealing with Oliver Cromwell's bloodthirsty military campaign in Ireland it had quoted Cromwell's justification for the massacre of 2000 defenceless people at Drogheda on 11th September 1649:

> "I am persuaded that this is a righteous judgment of God upon those barbarous wretches who have imbrued their hands with so much innocent blood."

The letter-writer had failed to grasp that these words, spoken by Laurence Olivier who was playing Cromwell, did not reflect the opinion of the British Broadcasting Corporation, which had compounded its offence by broadcasting them, no doubt deliberately, on the eve of the fatal anniversary. As far as he was concerned the Irish had been called bloodthirsty barbarians by Chatham and the scriptwriter, both of whom he said deserved to be "shot down like dogs", and in the next rather muddled paragraph, which also contained references to Queen's College Dublin and the potato famine, the writer explained that he proposed to do the shooting himself as soon as possible.

"Oh!" cried Miss Brown. "Susan, come and look at this."

*

The Director-General was out of London on some august business of his own. But by mid-morning the letter was on its way to Scotland Yard for examination by Special Branch, the experts on Irish terrorism, and the furor about Miss Brown's discovery had reached the highest BBC level available in Reith's absence.

"Have they contacted Chatham yet?" asked the Commodore.

"No," said the Colonel. "He's not in today. Nursing the wound in his arm, I think."

"They're still trying to contact him," said the ex-Governor of the Punjab.

The Director-General favoured ex-servicemen as his immediate subordinates. Considering their lack of radio expertise they were amazingly good at their jobs.

"How about the scriptwriter?" asked the Commodore. "He's threatened too."

But the scriptwriter, a freelance, had joined the International Brigade which was fighting a losing battle against Franco and his Nazi and Fascist backers in Spain.

"Rather embarrassing," murmured the ex-Governor of the Punjab. The Conservative press would seize on this fact as yet more evidence that the BBC was a hotbed of communism.

"We can forget him," the Commodore decided. "He'll be safe from Irish terrorists in the trenches round Madrid."

"Have to arrange protection for Chatham though," said the Colonel.

"Good Lord, yes," said the Commodore. "A very valuable man, gets the best out of his chaps. The sort of officer material we can't afford to lose."

"I *listen* to his stuff," the ex-Governor confessed.

"We can't take risks, let's send him on leave," the Colonel suggested. "Warren could take over."

The Commodore vetoed this. "Warren's hands are full with the Palace and the Christmas hook-up, he hasn't the time. Besides, Chatham's got pride, he wouldn't stand for skulking in a corner. Let's work out a really thorough protection drill . . ."

This was the sort of problem they understood and enjoyed. They spent twenty happy minutes working out an elaborate scheme.

"That's that," said the Commodore. "Next point, how do we handle this press-wise?"

"Have to soft-pedal the Irish angle," remarked the Colonel.

Back in the summer the IRA had mounted a bombing campaign during a royal visit to Ulster, and intelligence reports spoke of worse to come in the autumn. The Home Office had imposed a news blackout on reports of threatening Irish activities in England, allegedly in the interests of security but in fact because business confidence would be shaken by suggestions that a wave of bombings was imminent in London.

"Then we say nothing at all to the press about the letter?" asked the Colonel.

"By far the best course," said the ex-Governor heartily.

It was an attractive idea. If the letter was not mentioned to the press they could avoid admitting publicly that it had been lying around in PCU for four days before it was noticed. But the Commodore disagreed.

"No, that might be very unwise. You saw Harold Millbank's column yesterday?"

Harold Millbank was the radio columnist of a conservative paper with an unrelenting hate for the BBC. His current theme was that Reith was a power-crazed dictator and that discontent was rife among the staff.

"And now he's saying they're all at each other's throats quarrelling," the Commodore added.

"You're right," said the ex-Governor. "He'll say our chaps are shooting at each other unless we make it clear that the attack's coming from outside."

"Why not just say that Chatham's had a threatening letter from a listener?" the Colonel suggested. "No details. The Home Office can't object to that."

"Better get hold of Chatham first, though, and brief him," said the Commodore. "If the press ask him about the letter and he says he hasn't had it, our faces will be red."

"But where *is* Chatham?" said the ex-Governor impatiently.

*

43

Chatham's life had become uncomfortable. Before he finally left Vine Street the previous night, the police had advised him to make the unknown gunman's task more difficult by avoiding his usual haunts, spending the night at a friend's and coming and going at Broadcasting House as unobtrusively as possible. Inevitably, a shooting outside Vine Street Police Station had come to the ears of the crime reporters. There were stories in most of Friday morning's papers, some of them with a photograph, and he foresaw trouble evading the press.

There was nothing at Broadcasting House, he decided, which could not wait till Monday. So after a night spent with friends in Kensington and a few calls to the office, he slipped off to Paddington Station, bound for Fontbury. No doubt it was one of the "haunts" he ought to avoid, but he had to take the risk. Angela had left for Fontbury the previous night and he had to talk to her.

Arthur, the gardener who doubled as chauffeur, met his train at Reading with the ancient Lanchester limousine which was part of the Fontbury set-up. Encased pretentiously in glass, he was driven through quiet lanes, up the picturesque village street, and in at the elaborate wrought-iron gates which led to the carriage sweep. As he climbed out, he glanced up at the eighteenth-century house of grey Cotswold stone which he had been born in. Six months ago it had become his, quite unexpectedly. It was heartbreakingly beautiful. Despite his many troubles, the sight of it consoled him.

Harrison advanced across the entrance hall in a butlerish glide to take his hat and coat.

"Good morning, Mr Tony."

It was amusing how Harrison still said "Mr Tony" through habit, as though Chatham's father was still alive.

He answered Harrison's anxious queries about his arm and asked where Angela was.

"Madam left an hour ago."

"Left? To go where?"

"She didn't say, Mr Tony." Harrison's face had gone carefully blank. "She took a suitcase and told me she didn't know when she would be back. And there is a message from the BBC, asking you to ring urgently. You will find the details on the pad."

Chatham nodded and went to the morning room to telephone. The BBC could wait, though. He put through a call to his brother-in-law in Wiltshire.

"Gerald? Can I ask for a favour? People are taking pot shots at me—"

"So I gather."

"And I've been advised to stay away from my usual places, like the club and Fontbury. Would it be a frightful bore if I asked to lie low with you for the weekend?"

"Oh," said Gerald, sounding alarmed. "I'm not sure . . . I'll just check."

The telephone was covered up for a hasty consultation.

"Actually, Tony, it's a bit awkward," said Gerald, after a longish pause. "You see, Angela's here."

"I thought she might be. That's partly why I rang. I want to come and talk to her."

"Angela doesn't want to talk to you, she says. And frankly, old boy, I think it would be wiser if you stayed away from her for a bit. She's in a very edgy state."

"I know, that's why she's dreamed up this absurd story about me and my secretary."

"Absurd or not, she doesn't want to see you."

"Gerald, I hope you're not encouraging this divorce nonsense?"

"I prefer not to discuss that."

"My secretary is not and never has been pregnant. If the thing comes into court the evidence, so called, of my night of love in Manchester will be blown sky-high."

"So you say, old boy, so you say."

Chatham cut him off abruptly and reached for the message pad. Who was it at Broadcasting House that wanted him to ring?

To avoid being summarily ejected from his editorial chair Andrew Chisholm had found it necessary to share the view of the pro-prietor, and of several other Fleet Street proprietors, that the BBC was a squalid nuisance which stole bread from the mouths of honest journalists and ought not to exist. At his instigation the paper had made the most of the Talking Mongoose affair, in which the BBC had tried unwisely to intimidate a member of staff into not bringing a libel action which it thought might embarrass the Corporation. This provided the text for a spate of stories in which the whole staff was seen cringing in terror under the lash of the "Prussian" Director-General. The BBC was also chastised in the paper for abandoning the Baird television system, which depended on a crude mechanical scanner but was wholly British, in favour of EMI's cathode ray tube which gave far better results. But since EMI was half American the BBC was guilty of selling out British genius to sinister foreign interests. Worse still, it had culpably failed to spend money which it had not got and could not extract from the Treasury on a huge expansion of its tiny television service, which was necessary if the manufacturers were to sell more television sets.

And now a senior BBC producer was being shot at. Interesting. . . . He sent for Harold Millbank, the paper's radio columnist.

"Ah, Harold. You on to this Chatham thing?"

"Sure," said Millbank. "They're covering up as usual. 'Our Mr Chatham's had a threatening letter.' When? They're not sure, which means it lay about in that damn Programme Correspondence Unit for weeks before it was found. What's in it? They're not prepared to say, it would not be in the public interest. Why would it not be in the public interest? Press Relations doesn't know, it hasn't seen the letter. Where is Chatham? Press Relations knows, but has been instructed not to say. I have my spies out, though. I'll find him "

"What d'you think they're covering up?" asked Chisholm.

"Chatham's been rowing with his wife. She shot at him, and the Holy and Blessed Corporation has decided that the foul breath of scandal must not touch Chatham, who is a star turn and the darling of the highbrow critics. The threatening letter doesn't exist. They invented it to make the shooting look like an outside job by the lunatic fringe."

"Mm. What do the police say?"

"Vine Street's being tight-lipped too. There's a silly little pink public schoolboy from Hendon in charge, his first case, I should think. Does he suspect anyone? No. Does he know what's in the letter? He can't say. And when I ask him where the letter is, he looks like he's going to wet his pants and start to cry."

"Did he tell you where it was?"

"No, he got quite hysterical about it."

Chisholm thought for a moment. "Better go carefully on this one. There could be another explanation. Suppose the letter's at Special Branch? There's a Home Office stop on anything about Irish terrorism in London. If Chatham's broadcast something that got across the IRA, and they'd had a go at Chatham, the letter would be rushed round to Special Branch and everyone would clam up, even about where it is."

"No, I thought of that. I've been through the *Radio Times* for the past three months. His name hasn't been on anything controversial or even topical. All long-haired stuff."

"Here's another possibility, Harold. Someone in the BBC has it in for Chatham. It's quite likely, the place is a snake pit. Someone decides to shoot him up. So he concocts this threatening letter to put your pink schoolboy off the track."

"Ah," said Millbank. "I like that idea."

SIX

THE SPECIAL BRANCH man was not impressed by the Irishman's threatening letter. "It's nothing to do with the IRA," he announced. "It has the wrong feel."

The Commodore nodded. Special Branch had been set up in Victorian times to deal with Irish terrorism. They ought to know.

"It's not the IRA style, Commodore. It's got none of their usual trademarks."

"Then who sent it?"

"Possibly an unbalanced individual with an Irish background. It may be that, or it may be simply a fake. Some personal enemy of Chatham's who's decided to murder him and wants to put us off the scent."

"But who would want to murder Chatham?" asked the Commodore.

"You're better qualified to answer that than me."

"You mean, it could be someone in the BBC?" asked the Commodore nervously. It was quite possible, he realised. For instance, Drama Department hated Chatham for snatching the features output away from them, and most of the drama people were quite mad. Only the other day that extraordinary chap Val Gielgud had come to him wanting permission to broadcast a shocker of a play called "Ibsen's Ghosts" that his sisters hadn't been allowed to see, some dirty French farce by all accounts . . . BBC employees plotting to murder each other. If a hint of this reached the likes of Harold Millbank, the fat would be in the fire.

"Look, can't you keep this idea under your hat?" he asked. It was the obvious solution. If Special Branch went on treating the letter as genuine the security blackout on it would continue and Harold Millbank would never know.

After a lot of persuasion the Special Branch man agreed. But he took an even poorer view of two more typewritten death threats which arrived in Programme Correspondence Unit and were duly forwarded to him. Meanwhile, Vine Street was making little progress. The bullet which had passed through Chatham's arm had been found embedded in a tree trunk on the edge of Regent's Park. According to the ballistics laboratory it had been fired from a high velocity .475 rifle, and Detective-Sergeant Verney had been rebuked for not searching Imperial Mansions promptly for such a weapon. His laborious investigation of the other inhabitants of the block had revealed no obvious connection with Irish nationalism, the BBC or the Chathams. The case had come to a halt.

In Jennifer Howe's rare moments of leisure it had occurred to her that she ought logically to be in love with Chatham. She had rejected several suitors on finding that she could not take them at their own high valuation, but Chatham seemed to have no valuation of himself. He was too busy concentrating on his job, the people he worked with, the attempt to rescue his marriage. He had scrupulously refrained from appealing to her sympathy as an ill-used husband, and his unobtrusive good looks made one think at once, "What a nice man." Jennifer was acutely concerned for his safety and had a key role in the precautions surrounding him. But she was not in love with him.

Harold Millbank was taking an intense interest in Chatham from his own quite different angle. He had discovered that Chatham was back at work in Broadcasting House and was coming and going in a closed chauffeur-driven car which drove up to the service entrance in Langham Street with obvious plain-clothes men in attendance and two huge outside broadcast vans blocking the line of fire. The car had twice shaken off Millbank's pursuing taxi, but he traced it at last to Dolphin Square, a large block of flats in Pimlico with a lift from its underground garage, into which Chatham was driven at speed.

His secretary sounded charming on the phone, but she was quick-witted and impossible to get past. Millbank had a network of talkative contacts in Broadcasting House, and he had no difficulty in building up a detailed picture of Chatham's past and present activities. A colleague with a reliable source inside the servants' gossip network of Berkshire country houses was helping with the Fontbury angle. But the story was not developing. Days passed and nothing happened. The Vine Street public schoolboy squirmed and "could not say" whether more death threats had been received. Millbank was reduced to filling his column with yet another powerful plea for the expansion of the television service, in which he stated, correctly, that Broadcasting House dreaded the dawn of the television age and knew that the anarchic goings-on at Alexandra Palace were beyond its control or even comprehension.

The story dropped out of all the papers, except that one of the astrologers thought it a safe bet to predict, correctly as it turned out, the sudden death of "a person connected with the Portland Place area".

On the eve of the day when this prophecy was to be fulfilled, taxis were drawing up outside Broadcasting House and depositing the evening's load of speakers. The BBC broadcast as much as possible live. Recording equipment was expensive and the tension of live performance made for a better programme.

The celebrities emerging from the taxis were in evening dress. So were the people waiting for them in the entrance hall, the duty officer in a dinner jacket and the receptionists in long dresses. When told that this was carrying respectability to absurd lengths, the BBC would reply that evening dress was worn as a courtesy to the contributors, who would normally dress for dinner. It was dimly aware that people existed who ate in their shirt sleeves at half-past five. But they seldom broadcast and the question of courtesy to them did not arise.

In a windowless room on the eighth floor Peter Warren sat at the Dramatic Control Panel. He was sweating a little. In a few moments the engineers would switch him through to the long-wave transmitter at Droitwich and cue him. The Vasco da Gama feature would be on the air.

Working with a strange balance and control team had made him more nervous than usual. Chatham had failed, or perhaps not tried, to get Music Executive to relent and let him use their own. During the midday break in the rehearsal he and Chatham had

had a very public row about this. In the afternoon his mind was not on what he was doing, and he had rubbed the unfamiliar balance and control team up the wrong way.

One of the junior engineers, a dark athletic-looking young man with smelly brilliantine on his hair, annoyed him particularly. He could not think why, but had deliberately flustered the young man with a quick series of complicated instructions, then said something sarcastic which made the whole team sulk. The show was badly under-rehearsed.

The engineers in Central Control Room buzzed through. A million or more people spread throughout Britain were waiting. He cued the Theatre Orchestra, which was in a studio two floors below. The opening music began coming through the loudspeaker beside the control panel.

Four floors below Warren, the Narrator sat waiting in a cubicle off one of the studios to be used by the actors. There were three of them, according to whether the scene to be played called for a bright, a dull or a neutral acoustic. The Narrator's cue light came on. "Vasco da Gama," he began. "An evocation of the age of discovery . . ."

Down at the control panel the mixer, sitting beside Warren, faded down the orchestra and held it under the Narrator's voice.

In yet another studio on a different floor, a speaking chorus of Common People was waiting to make its contribution. Warren could see none of the forces he was controlling. It was BBC doctrine that a producer who could see into the studios during a dramatic production would be unduly influenced by what he saw and would make misjudgments. In radio the effect should be judged by ear alone.

The actors, headed by a middle-aged lady who specialised in doing children, launched into the first scene, which dealt with Vasco da Gama's upbringing. The dark young engineer had nothing to do at the moment and stood looking over the shoulder of his senior colleague on the panel. What was it that made him so dislikeable? A reminder of some unpleasant experience, Warren thought, a resemblance to some person he had disliked . . .

Vasco da Gama had now grown up, and started to enlist

51

financial backing for his voyage of discovery. "We've lost forty seconds," said the girl with the stopwatch. "That last scene was very slow. D'you want them speeded up?"

Warren snapped back to attention. If they overran, it would affect the timing of the main evening news. One of the actors was being very portentous and heavy, and it was infecting the others. Someone would have to go up to the next floor and make the circular hand signal which meant "speed up".

"George can go," suggested the control engineer on the panel.

The dark young man nodded and slipped out.

George. He was called George. Suddenly the truth hit Warren. It wasn't a resemblance that had puzzled him. It was the two-year difference in age, the difference between a boy of eighteen and a man of twenty.

"What's that chap's name?" he asked.

"George Otway," said the control engineer coldly. "He's very quick and capable when he's given a chance."

Otway. Warren felt physically ill. An ugly chunk of his past had just caught up with him. Young Otway had given no sign of recognition, but must surely know who he was.

The girl with the stopwatch was staring at him in alarm. Vasco da Gama seemed to have stopped in its tracks.

"Cue studio six," he said hastily.

The Chorus of Common People, segregated in its distant studio, was already impersonating a cheerful crowd in a market place. This was to be faded under an encounter between two of Vasco da Gama's backers, who would explain to each other and the listeners his plan for a voyage round the world. But the unexpected was now happening.

"My son, do not venture upon the storm-tossed seas," intoned an actress above the market chatter of the Common People.

"Mother, I must!" cried an actor raptly.

"Do not hazard yourself among the towers of ice," moaned another actor.

"Father, I must!"

The man at the gramophone turntables shuffled the pages of his script. "Hey, what's happening, I'm lost."

Disaster. Warren had cued the wrong studio. A whole chunk of essential explanation had been left out.

"The next cue's the seagull," said the man on grams. "D'you want it or not?"

"Yes," said Warren desperately. Anything to give him time to think.

The seagull recording was meant to set the scene at a quayside for Vasco da Gama's embarkation. But the listeners had not yet been told where he was going or why. The missing sequence would have to be shoved in somewhere quick. He scribbled hasty instructions to the actors, and sent everyone available scurrying away to the studios with them.

"That enough of the seagull?" asked the man on grams, preparing to lift the needle from the disc.

"Yes, cue the Chorus studio," said Warren.

The seagull ended its performance and the Chorus of Common People began to recite in unison:

"Our lot is hard, our station is humble.
We till the soil
And know nothing of the doings of Kings.
But today is different.
The sails unfurl and for a moment
Our lives are touched by the stir of great events . . ."

"What do we do when this finishes?" asked the engineer on the control panel.

"Go back to the seagull," said Warren in agony.

The BBC seagull was a standing joke with the critics. It was such an easy, evocative way of establishing a seaside atmosphere that it sometimes appeared four or five times in the same week; it was far more over-exposed than any popular broadcaster. But the actors were all in the wrong places, having positioned themselves in studios with the right acoustic for their next scene, not the one they ought to have played three minutes before. They had to be given time to regroup.

After an eternity of confusion and seagull squawks everyone needed for the missing scene was assembled in one studio, the chorus resumed its market chatter and the production got going again. But there were still problems. When they returned to the quayside there must be no more seagull and the chorus must be prevented from repeating its long complaint that its lot was hard. The stopwatch girl had rushed from studio to studio with messages and had lost count of time. Clearly they were running very late. Something (but what, and how much?) would have to be cut if they were not to commit the awful crime of delaying the news bulletin . . .

When it was all over and Warren was left with his thoughts in the deserted control room, they were not pleasant. Having made a fool of himself in front of the studio technicians and a huge unseen audience was not the worst of it. Nor was the damage he had probably done to his career prospects. From his personal and professional point of view, George Otway could not have popped up out of his past at a more awkward time.

By common consent the balance and control team adjourned to the Stag's Head to restore its shattered nerves. They were a close-knit group. Most of them had been radio operators in the Merchant Navy or cinema musicians before joining the BBC. They drank their beer in pints.

"Warren made a dog's breakfast of that," said Ed Bridgeman, the senior engineer who had done miracles of rescue work on the control panel.

Everyone began to comment.

"Wasn't concentrating, was he?"

"On a show like that you need to keep your temper."

"That row with Chatham in the dinner break. Such language."

"It was real nasty what he said to George too."

"He had no call to pick on George like he did."

"You had dealings with him before, George?"

They all looked at Otway. It struck them that he had been very silent ever since he left Broadcasting House, and was looking miserable. Ed Bridgeman gave an unobtrusive nod. He was the team leader and George, the youngest member, was under his wing. The others talked of something else, then moved away tactfully to join another group.

"Worried, lad?" Ed asked.

"Aye. He'll make trouble for me."

"No fear, if he tries to I'll show them my log entry: 'Transmission disorganised owing to producer cueing wrong studio'."

George shook his head doubtfully. After a silence Ed prompted: "You and him had words before, then?"

"Aye. I give him the hell of a thrashing once." George paused shamefacedly. "On account of my sister."

Ed knew at once that this went deep. He and George came from the same type of background, from chapel-going families struggling along just above the poverty line and clinging fiercely to their good name because it was almost all they had.

"Playing about with her, is he?" Ed asked gently.

"She's dead. There was a baby coming."

This was a drastically condensed version of the truth. Warren had given Annie Otway a good time, got her with child, then handed her the price of a back-street abortion. Whoever she went to had botched the job, panicked and dumped the body on Wimbledon Common. The thought of the inquest and the publicity still made George hot all over. The Otway family in its shame never mentioned that time even to each other.

But Ed Bridgeman was a good listener. George soon found himself telling how Warren had come to the house a few days before the inquest. "First he offered us a lot of money to keep his name out of it. My dad turned that down flat. Then he said he didn't know about the baby and having it got rid of and he wasn't the father anyway because she was a loose woman who went with lots of men; and that's what he'd say at the inquest if we made trouble for him. So my dad said we'd keep quiet, on account of not blackening Annie's name more than we had to. But it wasn't true, not about the other men. It was just that he had money and she wanted a good time." George paused. "You'll not tell the others?"

"Not if you'd rather."

55

"That was how I come to give him a thrashing. I was that angry when he went away from the house, I followed him down the road and went for him, a real do it was, knocked out some of his teeth and all."

"Did you know he was in the BBC?" Ed asked.

"Aye, but I thought it was okay. I was in the lift with him once soon after I joined, and he looked straight through me, didn't know me from Adam. Mind you I've changed a bit. I was babyish-looking at eighteen."

Ed lifted up his pint, but held it halfway to his mouth without drinking. "Don't look round. Warren's just come in."

"Going to join us, is he?"

"He's buying himself a drink. Maybe he will." After a broadcast producers often thought it diplomatic to join the engineers they had been working with for a drink. But Warren was still standing by himself at the bar, looking disgruntled.

"Why d'you reckon he'll make trouble for you, George?" Ed asked. "He was dead scared when I told him your name, that was why he made a cock-up of the production. He must realise the situation. He makes trouble for you, you make trouble for him."

"They'd listen to him, not me. He'd say I made it up, I've no proof."

"If I was him," Ed reasoned, "I'd come over here and say to you straight: leave me alone and I'll leave you alone."

"Then why doesn't he?"

Ed stole another look. "He's watching you, George. Maybe he does want a quiet word with you. You game to let him?"

"Aye, if he wants to."

"Me and the others better go back, it's almost time. Give him a chance to get you alone. Don't worry if it makes you a few minutes late, we'll cover for you."

George stayed, casting glances at Warren from time to time. But Warren made no move and he was damned if he would make an approach himself. He began to be impatient. He was on the late shift, he ought to be on duty now. But before he could finish his pint comfortably he would have to pumpship. He pushed his way through the crowd to the urinal.

Warren watched him go. He had come to the Stag's Head knowing that it was the balance and control people's usual haunt. His idea had been to tackle Otway and persuade him somehow to keep his mouth shut, but after what he had seen that would obviously not do. When he came in Otway and Ed Bridgeman were in earnest conference well away from the rest of the team, and from the way they reacted when they saw him it was clear that they were discussing him. Otway had probably told Bridgeman the whole story already, to judge from the ostentatious way he had marched out, taking the rest of the team with him. Creating the opportunity for a tête-à-tête obviously. Afterwards he would ask Otway what had been said and the whole story would be engineering department gossip in no time. Decidedly, he would not talk the thing out with Otway. There was another solution, much better, it had come to him in a flash. He finished his drink and went back to the bar.

"Two whiskies. Doubles."

When Otway came back Warren was nowhere to be seen. There was no point in staying, so he gulped down the rest of his pint and made for the door, thinking vaguely that the aftertaste of his brown ale was rather odd.

Out in the street the cold air hit him. Before he had gone twenty yards he felt dizzy and very ill. He staggered about for a time, then clung to some railings hoping that the dizziness would pass. It did not.

Through a gap in the railings some steps led down to a basement area. Rather than make an exhibition of himself in the street he half fell, half stumbled down the steps and sat down at the bottom. Presently he fell asleep.

When the cold air woke him he felt even worse. If he had been a more experienced drinker he would have recognised the taste of whisky. He would also have known that the only way of getting rid of that lethal mixture, a whisky chaser, was to put two fingers down his throat and rid his stomach of it. Instead he stood up unsteadily and started to look for Broadcasting House. He must get there, he was on the late shift. Presently he found it and steered a wavering course across the entrance hall into a lift in which he collapsed. In the morning he was sacked out of hand for being drunk on duty.

SEVEN

"WHAT DID YOU say to him, George lad?" asked Ed Bridgeman.

"What could I say? He just gave me my cards and told me to go."

"Now listen, George. Everyone has the right to appeal to the Director-General if they think they've been done wrong. I'll speak for you, so will the supervisor. Soon as you get home, you sit down now and write a letter to him."

"What will I put in it?"

"You beg to apologise for what happened last night and respectfully ask for your dismissal to be reconsidered, the fact being that someone put whisky in your pint for a joke—"

"Whisky? Was that what it was?"

"Must have been, to put you out like that."

"Why don't I say it was Warren did it?"

"No, no, keep Warren out of it, only put their backs up, that would. Unless you had proof positive they'd take his side."

"But he'll speak against me."

"His opinion won't be asked. His department's not concerned."

"I reckon I'll talk to him all the same."

"Better not, lad," Ed decided. With George in his present mood a meeting between them might develop into a brawl which would endanger his appeal. "But cheer up, lad," he went on. "They're good employers on the whole, they listen to reason. We'll get you your job back, never fear."

George forced a disbelieving smile, collected his belongings and left Broadcasting House.

Up on the fifth floor Chatham was discussing a projected feature on the philosophy of education with Bertrand Russell. The telephone rang, and Jennifer answered it. "I'm afraid he has someone with him at the moment," she said softly.

59

"It's very urgent, Miss," said the distant voice.

"Who's speaking, please?"

"Harrison, Miss. Mr Chatham's butler."

"One moment, please."

Jennifer interrupted the conference, and was told to say that Chatham would ring back as soon as possible. But this, it seemed, would not do.

"He says he's not at Fontbury House," she reported. "He's in the phone box in the village."

Chatham excused himself and picked up the phone. "What's the trouble, Harrison?"

"Oh Mr Tony, I'm sorry to disturb you at business, but we're all at sixes and sevens here. Mrs Chatham's come back from her brother's. She's packing all her clothes and a lot of other stuff too, the silver from the dining room and so on. She's very excited and acting strange, I think she's been drinking."

"I see," murmured Chatham, glancing uneasily at Britain's most eminent philosopher.

"She says she's made arrangements to ... divorce you, Mr Tony."

"Yes. I hope it won't come to that."

"I had to phone you, sir, Mrs Chatham said I'd been disrespect-ful to her and ordered me out of the house. I said no, I took my orders from you not her, and she started throwing things at me, the Worcester china and so on, some of it's broken. I didn't know what to do for the best, so I came to the village to phone."

"I'm sorry to hear this, Harrison. I'd better come down straight away."

"And what shall I do, Mr Tony? Go back to the house?"

Chatham hesitated. "That might make things worse. Why don't you spend the night at your sister's in Reading and I'll contact you there in the morning? Don't worry, Harrison. I'll start down to Fontbury at once."

He turned to Bertrand Russell. "I do apologise. My wife's been taken ill, would you mind awfully if we went on with this some other time?"

The philosopher expressed concern and withdrew. Jennifer had already run through the rest of the day's arrangements, deciding what could be postponed and what needed tidying up before he left.

"The Galileo script. I ought to start typing it soon if it's wanted for Friday."

"Oh Lord! I was working on it last night at home—or rather in that horrible little Pimlico hide-out they've put me in. Let's see . . . Yes, I'll have to go there to pick up my car. D'you mind coming there with me? Then I can give it you to bring back."

"Of course. I'll get my coat."

The chauffeur-driven hire car was waiting at the service entrance. Despite the lapse of time the thorough precautions taken for Chatham's safety had not been relaxed. The same car was never used on two consecutive days. There were three of them, from a firm connected with a detective agency. All had blind rear quarters so that a passenger on the back seat could not be seen.

Chatham sat hunched and silent in his corner till they were half-way through Mayfair, when he sat up abruptly. "God, Jennifer! I never thought. They might attack the car, I had no right to expose you to the risk."

She had already thought about this, and reached conclusions. "I don't suppose anything will happen. It hasn't for almost a week."

"I shall soon ask for all this fuss to stop. My lunatic Irishman seems to have changed his mind."

"Oh, but you mustn't!" cried Jennifer, then wished she had sounded less vehement.

"Why not?"

"He may be waiting till you're off your guard to try again," she said in a more detached tone. "Or . . . shooting you didn't work, he may try something more elaborate that takes time to mount."

The car nose-dived down a ramp into the underground car park of Dolphin Square.

"Wait here a moment," said Chatham and hurried away to the lift. When he came back he had an overnight bag and the rough draft of the Galileo script, which he handed to her. The chauffeur held the car door open, ready to drive him to the station.

"No, I'm going down by road, my car's over there."

"Should you?" said Jennifer. "Your arm . . ."

"It's almost healed, I can manage." He turned to the chauffeur. "I want you to make a dummy run, empty, back to Broadcasting House. Anyone watching will think I'm with you and follow, then I can get away."

"I could have gone with him," said Jennifer as the hire car disappeared up the ramp into the daylight.

"No. I'd have worried." He went over to a large sports car further down the garage, and deposited his overnight bag in it.

"Should you be going to Fontbury at all?" asked Jennifer. "They might be waiting there for you."

He looked at her rather coldly. "I'm very fond of my wife. She's going through a bad patch, and I have to help her." He pulled money out of his wallet. "Now let's get the hall porter to call you a cab."

"I'm perfectly capable of finding a cab for myself," she said. She was angry, but with herself, not him. She was not in love with him. By fussing idiotically about his safety she had convinced him that she was.

George Otway stood on the pavement outside Broadcasting House, watching the entrance and waiting for Warren to come out. It was lunch time. People he knew by sight were pouring out of the building, which was forbidden territory now.

It was all very well Ed Bridgeman telling him to keep away from Warren. He was too angry for that. Warren had got him sacked. Warren must damn well get him his job back, or else.

Luckily Warren came out of the building alone. Nothing much could have been said in front of a witness. He saw George at once, realised that it meant trouble, and turned away to hurry up Portland Place.

George fell in step beside him. "Excuse me, Mr Warren, I'd like a word with you."

"Would you now? Too bad, I'm in a hurry."

"I'll walk along with you then," said George, as Warren quickened his pace. "You had no call to play that trick on me, lose me my job. I wasn't doing you any harm."

Warren turned and faced him. "I cannot imagine what you can possibly be talking about."

"You bloody can. I'm talking about you and Annie. I'm telling you it's all over and forgotten, you've no call to pick on me like that."

"Please try to bloody grasp that you've mistaken me for someone else."

"No, Mr Warren. If you want another thrashing you're going the right way about it."

"Taxi!" shouted Warren, causing a passing cab to make a U-turn.

"You leave me alone, I leave you alone," cried George.

"Admirable. First class. You've got the right idea at last," snapped Warren, climbing into the cab. "Five, Princess of Wales Avenue, Battersea, driver."

"No, you don't, you slimy bastard," George yelled, trying to climb in after him.

Warren kicked him hard in the belly, but George grabbed his foot and started dragging him out of the cab. Warren landed a blow with his free foot in George's groin. As George staggered back across the pavement Warren slammed the cab door and it drove off.

"Annoying you, was he?" the cabby asked.

"Unemployed. Expected me to wave my damn wand like a magician and get him a job." Warren was very satisfied with his handling of the Otway problem. The wretched young man had hardly any nuisance value now, the BBC would not listen to slanderous nonsense from an ex-employee who had been sacked for drunkenness.

The cab drew up outside Five, Princess of Wales Avenue, a late-Victorian block of flats with a row of more recently built lock-up garages behind it. He gave the straight-eight Delage inside it a nod of satisfaction. The bodywork was coachbuilt, a silver-grey drophead coupé. The King was at Royal Lodge in Windsor Great Park. His appointment was at two-thirty. He tucked his shirt inside his trouser-band, tidied himself generally and started up the Delage.

But as he drove off down the narrow driveway along the side of the block, the exit to the street was barred by a taxi which had just drawn up. Someone was paying it off. Otway.

Otway had seen him and came running toward the Delage. A few yards in front of its long, high bonnet he stood stock still, blocking its escape to the street.

Warren let down the window. "Get out of the way or I'll run you down." But Otway stood his ground, shouting abuse. Warren was in a panic. He cursed himself for having got flustered and given the Battersea address to his cabby in Otway's hearing. What would the King think if he arrived at Royal Lodge covered with blood and with half his teeth broken? There was no time to pacify this rampant young bully, it would make him late for the appointment. His temples were throbbing with anger, but he had enough self-control not to slap in the clutch and crush his enemy under the Delage's low-slung chassis. Instead he edged it slowly forward till it was almost touching Otway.

Grinning fiercely, Otway laid a hand on the shining radiator, and did not step aside.

Warren let in the clutch again. The car inched forward with Otway withdrawing little by little in front of it.

Presently George took a quick look round. He had been forced out into the roadway. Warren would soon have room for man-oeuvre to dodge past him. He made a dash for the driver's door, intending to wrench it open and drag Warren out. But the Delage's bonnet was yards long, the bodywork was tiny by comparison. By the time he reached the driver's door Warren had put his foot down and the car surged forward. He would have broken every bone in his fingers if he tried to grab the doorhandle.

As Warren drove out of London to the West he tried to think about what he would say to the King. But an unpleasant fact of life kept surfacing; the Otway problem was far more serious than he had thought.

At half past four Jennifer decided to give her typewriter a rest from Galileo and began tidying up some loose ends. One of them was a query over a *Radio Times* billing for a feature of Peter Warren's. Lavinia would have the answer.

Lavinia's office door was half open. She was talking in a low, confidential tone into the telephone.

". . . A pink folder? Yes. He locks his desk, but I know where there's a spare key. . .No, no, dear, she'd see through that in a flash, she's quite a brainy little thing, I'll think of a better excuse . . . One moment, dear, the damn door's open."

She kicked it shut with a heel. Jennifer heard no more and went back to her office, wondering what would happen next.

Presently Lavinia put her head round the door. "Jennifer, my angel, are you fiendishly busy? I'll buy you a rope of pearls if you'll do something for me."

"For diamonds I'd consider it."

"No, no dear, diamonds are only for when the proposal's immoral. Could you get these discs from Gramophone Library, Peter wants to listen to them tomorrow and choose the theme music for 'Night Train'?"

Jennifer took the long list. "They'll take ages to look all these out."

"I know, dear, but could you stand there and make hideous faces at them so that they hurry? If you just leave them the list they'll get round to it next Tuesday week."

"Oh . . . very well."

"I'd go myself but Manchester's supposed to be phoning back about some shepherds with understandable accents for the Christmas hook-up."

Jennifer made off towards the lifts, not very surprised to discover that the mysterious special relationship between Lavinia and Peter Warren involved spying on Chatham. She let two or three minutes pass before returning for the handbag she had carefully forgotten. Lavinia's office was empty and the door of her own, which she had left open, was shut.

A quarrel with Lavinia would complicate life. If possible she would avoid it without betraying Chatham's interests. She would pick up her handbag and say casually, "Can I help you find anything?" or something neutral like that.

She opened the door. There was no need to say anything. Lavinia lay sprawled on the office floor with a bullet through her head.

EIGHT

"So that's what she looks like nowadays, poor thing," mused Detective-Constable Burton as he gazed down into the dead face of Lavinia Mannerton. He remembered her, of course. Just after the war it must have been, for about three years you could hardly open one of the popular picture papers without coming across her photo. Amid fierce competition from other publicity-conscious society girls, she had come out on top as deb of the year, and that took personality as well as looks.

But she was no society beauty now, even if you ignored the bullet hole in her close-cropped head. Burton was not surprised at the ravaged lines of her face. He knew a lot about what had happened after she dropped out of the gossip columns.

One of the drawers of Chatham's desk was open. "Must have been looking for something in the desk," he remarked to Detective-Sergeant Verney. "She'd be bending forward, that would bring her head opposite—"

They both looked at the star-shaped hole in the window pane.

"The electric light was behind her. It was on when we came in," said Verney excitedly. "And she had short hair—an Eton crop. *Someone mistook her for Chatham.*"

"Yes, sarge," said Burton, who had reached this conclusion some minutes earlier.

"Where was she shot from, though? Not from street level."

"Not unless she was standing on the table with her head on one side."

Verney looked out of the window into the gloom of a showery autumn afternoon. "What's that building opposite?"

"The Langham Hotel, sarge."

They examined the grimy brick bulk of the hotel with its serried ranks of vaguely Gothic windows.

"Any of those bedrooms," said Burton.

"I'd better go over there, don't you think? But which floor d'you reckon she was shot from?"

Burton looked from the hole in the window to Lavinia, then rummaged in Chatham's desk till he found a ruler. "Measure her?"

Verney did so. "Five foot three."

Burton took back the ruler and measured the high heels of Lavinia's shoes, which had fallen off. "Say five feet five, but she was bending forward. Have to make allowances for that."

They measured the distance from the bullet hole in the window to the floor. "Horizontal or from above, if you ask me," Burton concluded. "Not from lower down."

Opposite, lights were on behind drawn curtains in a few of the bedrooms, but most of the windows were in darkness.

"Fourth or fifth floor," said Burton.

"Yes, I think so too. You wait here and deal with the photographers and all that, and I'll go over there. Try to get a statement from the girl who found her."

But the BBC officials who were hovering helpfully did not immediately produce Jennifer. She had been whisked off to the Features Executive office suite to receive moral support. "I know it's been a shock to you, Jennifer," said Miss Proctor. "But we must all try to keep calm."

Helping the creative workers to keep calm after a murder seemed to be among the functions of Features Executive.

"Put your head between your legs if you want to," said Miss Proctor encouragingly.

"Thank you. It was a shock, but I'm not going to faint."

"Sensible girl." But under her dabs of rouge and eye make-up Miss Proctor looked disappointed.

"Now, Jennifer. In a few minutes I expect the police will want to question you, and you need to think carefully what to say."

"Surely telling the truth is quite simple?"

"Of course, but the police won't thank you for a lot of chatter about things that aren't relevant."

"I don't quite understand," said Jennifer.

"For instance, we all know that poor Lavinia Mannerton was a hopelessly inefficient secretary. Mr Warren insisted on bringing her in from outside, quite against my advice. I can't think how he put up with her."

Jennifer said nothing, though she had often wondered about that herself.

"But it doesn't look nice to speak ill of the dead," Miss Proctor went on. "And it's very important not to tell outside people things that might give them a poor impression of the Corporation."

"You're suggesting that if I'm asked what sort of a person Lavinia was I should give a wholly favourable picture regardless of the facts?"

"Well, she is the tragic victim of a mistake," said Miss Proctor, as if seeing an imaginary newspaper headline. "Whoever shot her through the window was having another try at killing Mr Chatham, her shortcomings aren't relevant, you see."

Jennifer thought about this. "You may be right, but there's one thing about Lavinia that I'll have to tell the police. I happened to overhear a telephone conversation—"

"Oh dear," said Miss Proctor.

"—between Lavinia and someone who I suppose could have been Mr Warren, though I didn't hear her mention any name—"

"This is gossip, Jennifer, I don't want to hear."

"—a few minutes before Lavinia was shot."

Miss Proctor's bedaubed face froze. "Go on."

"To judge from Lavinia's replies, the other person was asking her to make an excuse and get me out of Mr Chatham's office, then go in there and search for some document that the other person wanted."

"Spying on Mr Chatham? Why on earth d'you imagine that Mr Warren would want to do that?"

"As you know, they were on very bad terms."

"You're not proposing to tell the police *that*, I hope. I never heard such a rigmarole. You've let your imagination run riot on a perfectly innocent conversation which you half heard and mis-understood."

"In that case," said Jennifer, "why did Lavinia come to me a few minutes later with a long list of gramophone records she said were urgently wanted and would I please get them? She knew the library clerks would take hours to look them out."

"Simple. She was too lazy to go herself, and too inefficient to send the list down in advance so that the records would be ready to collect. As for Mr Warren spying on Mr Chatham, I'm disappointed in you, Jennifer. I thought you were a steady, sensible girl."

Miss Proctor thought, drumming her fingers on the table. "Wait here a moment," she said, and hurried out.

While she was gone Jennifer thought about all the things that needed doing, and wondered if anyone was attending to them. Chatham ought to be phoned at Fontbury and told that Lavinia had died in his place. It would be a shock, especially if the news was broken to him in the form of a demand for comment from the press. Warren should know too, it would look bad if he was found carousing in some pub with his secretary lying dead.

Miss Proctor did not return. Instead Features Executive himself, whose underling she was, appeared and swept Jennifer into the inner office.

"The police," he began, "are convinced that this unfortunate woman was shot from outside the building in mistake for Mr Chatham."

"It seems the obvious conclusion," said Jennifer.

He nodded. "Now in making statements to the police . . . Jennifer, that's right, isn't it? . . . one has to remember that sooner or later a great deal of what you say will find its way into the newspapers, most of which are only too ready to seize on any minor detail which they can twist into a story discreditable to the Corporation. That is why we ask you to weigh beforehand very carefully what you say."

"Of course," said Jennifer. "I shall be careful to tell the exact truth."

"Er—yes. But about this rather dramatic story of yours about a telephone conversation which you say you half overheard between Miss Mannerton and Mr Warren—"

"Excuse me. I don't know that it was Mr Warren at the other end, though it seems likely."

"Who else would ask Miss Mannerton to look for something in Mr Chatham's office? I'm sure we'll find a simple explanation, some fact or figure that he wanted from Mr Chatham's files. Irresponsible statements about tension between the two could merely put the police on the wrong track."

"You're not suggesting that I suppress all mention of this phone call?"

"Oh dear me, no, of course not. But are you *quite* sure you would not be misleading the police if you told them it was furtive and conspiratorial in character? There are reasons which need not concern you, I might almost say reasons of state, why Mr Warren's name must not be touched by any breath of scandal."

Meaning his visits to the Palace, Jennifer thought. But she was not supposed to know about that.

"*Must* you hint at a conspiracy when you are questioned by the police? It isn't really relevant."

"On the contrary, it's highly relevant," Jennifer burst out. "Suppose a murderer wanted to get Lavinia into Mr Chatham's office so that he could shoot her—"

'Why can he not shoot her in her own office?"

"Because it's on the opposite side of the building. He phones Lavinia and asks her to look for something in Mr Chatham's desk, but he has to add: 'Don't tell his secretary, get her out of the way.' Otherwise she'd come to me and say, 'So-and-so has asked me to look for such-and-such' and I'd help her find it. So when she'd been shot I'd know who phoned."

"Oh dear, this is all very fanciful stuff. Two attempts have been made to shoot Mr Chatham. This was a third attempt, in which Miss Mannerton was shot by mistake."

"It looks like that," Jennifer said. "But it's all very puzzling. The police will have to decide in the light of all the evidence, including mine."

Features Executive looked at her with an expression of suppressed hatred. "All I can say is, when you are questioned I advise you, in your own interest, not to let your imagination run riot."

"You say 'in my own interest'. Are you suggesting that my BBC career will suffer if I tell the police what I believe to be the truth?"

"Oh dear me, no, what a shocking suggestion. But I think you should remember that steadiness and loyalty to the Corporation are among the qualities we look for in those, and I hope you are one of them, who can be considered for promotion from General Office to more senior posts."

Detective-Constable Burton had installed himself behind Peter Warren's desk. He was as heavily built as Warren, Jennifer decided, but much more organised-looking. He seemed cross, probably at her delay in presenting herself for questioning. But that was hardly her fault.

"Ah, there you are, Miss. I'll have some questions for you, and I'd like to have a word with this Mr Warren that the deceased lady worked for, but no one seems to know where he is."

"I think he had some outside engagements this afternoon. That's his desk diary in front of you."

Burton opened it. "Two-thirty. Christmas preparations. What's that?"

"Oh, it's what he puts when he's going to see the King about broadcasting his Christmas message. It's supposed to be confidential, but I expect it's all right you knowing."

"H'm. Then he'll have spent the afternoon at the Palace," said Burton stolidly.

"No, I heard Lavinia say he'd been told at the last minute to go to Royal Lodge. He was rather cross about it."

"Twenty past five," said Burton. "He'll not be there still?"

"No, but wasn't he going on somewhere?"

He looked at the desk diary again. "Five p.m. Coghill . . . Exeter, the next word looks like, but he'd never get there in the time."

"No, it's short for Exeter College Oxford, I remember now. If we put through a call quickly we'll catch him."

While they waited for the call to come through Burton asked her what Warren was doing in Oxford.

"Consulting someone who's an authority on Chaucer, they're thinking of doing a series in modern English . . . Hullo, Exeter

72

College? Dr Coghill's rooms, please . . . Good evening, Dr Coghill, this is the BBC here. I'm sorry to trouble you, but I believe Mr Warren is with you. Could I please have a word with him? It's Mr Chatham's secretary.'

Warren came on the line. "Jennifer? What's the trouble?"

He sounded so cheerful and confident that she felt suddenly tongue-tied. "Something quite horrible has happened . . . Look, there's a policeman here, I'd better hand you over to him."

While Burton broke the news in his down-to-earth voice, Jennifer took stock. After arriving at Royal Lodge at two-thirty, Warren could not possibly have shot Lavinia in London at four-thirty and kept an appointment at five in Oxford. So that disagreeable possibility was out of the way . . . But if Warren was not the murderer the phone call could hardly have been from him. From whom, then?

"He'll be back in London by eight," Burton reported as he put down the phone. "Quite distressed he was, as if he was very attached to his secretary. Were they . . . you know what I mean, Miss?"

"I doubt it," said Jennifer coldly. "He's quite a bit younger than Lavinia."

"I'm sorry, Miss, we have to ask these questions." He opened his notebook. "Now about when you found the body—"

"One moment," Jennifer interrupted. "Mr Chatham will be horribly upset when he hears what's happened. Has anyone told him?"

Burton doubted it, and muttered something to the effect that no one in the BBC seemed to know where anyone else was.

"He's gone down to Fontbury, his house in the country," she said. "His wife's ill or something. He must be there by now."

On Burton's instructions she rang him there. But Mrs Chatham, sounding even madder than usual, said he had left again for London twenty minutes earlier. Burton therefore left a message for him with the hall porter at Dolphin Square.

Meanwhile Jennifer had remembered something. Chatham had sent his chauffeur-driven car back to Broadcasting House empty, to deceive any watcher who might otherwise follow him to Fontbury. "So if anyone was spying on him," she told Burton, "they'd think he was back here at Broadcasting House."

Had Lavinia been shot in mistake for Chatham? If so, how did the phone call fit in? When the time came to tell Burton about it she repeated Lavinia's exact words as far as she could remember them and refused to be drawn into speculation about who the caller could have been if not Warren. Asked about relations between him and Chatham, she could not bring herself to peddle the official line that their relations were as peaceful and harmonious as those of David and Jonathan. But she tried not to over-dramatise.

"They fought a bit," she told Burton. "There was a row about a week ago."

"What was that about, please?"

"A technical matter to do with studio facilities."

Happily he did not ask for details, thus sparing her the daunting task of making the row about Music Executive's tiresome behaviour comprehensible to a policeman.

When she had made her statement Burton let her go and sat thinking, but not about what he had just heard. A personal problem confronted him. He was having a disagreeable trip down memory lane.

Sergeant Goddard, his old station sergeant at Vine Street. Put in charge of the vice squad by the super, in an area with about two hundred so-called night clubs in it. And then they were surprised when they found that Goddard, who earned six pounds a week, had a Chrysler and a two-thousand-pound house in Streatham and a safe deposit with a lot of cash in it. And some of the notes had been traced back to that old harridan Kate Meyrick.

Mrs Meyrick, the night club queen. Proctor's in Gerrard Street. The Silver Slipper in Regent Street. Both notorious for their tolerance of prostitution and drug peddling, but protected by massive payments to Goddard.

It was under Kate Meyrick's wing that Lavinia Mannerton had sought excitement when the debutante scene began to pall. She was an earl's granddaughter and influence had kept her name out of the papers. Sergeant Goddard had been well rewarded for keeping her out of the police courts.

When the scandal broke in 1928 Burton was questioned gently, because no one was keen to make the thing bigger than it had to be. But he was a friend of Goddard's and it was fairly obvious he had had his cut. That was why he was still a constable nine years later.

Here was the problem. He had a lot more detailed knowledge about Lavinia Mannerton's past than he could have come by in the course of duty. He knew because he had been up to the neck in the Goddard business, and he did not want to stir up memories of that. With an understanding detective-sergeant he could have passed on the information without being asked awkward questions. But with a pure-minded little squirt like Verney it was unthinkable.

Yet Lavinia Mannerton's past was at the centre of the whole case. The episode of the mysterious phone call proved that. It was unlucky for the murderer that it had been overheard. He had faked up an Irish scare with his anonymous letters and blooded Chatham without killing him. Why? Because if everyone thought the shot through the window was meant for Chatham, nobody would ask themselves who would want to murder Lavinia Mannerton, and why.

NINE

Colonel and Mrs Robertson, Bognor Regis. Signor Ettore Martinaggi, Milan. Hiram B. Hecht, Denver, Colorado. Sir Edward and Lady Campbell, Glenmurchan Lodge, Pitlochry. Mr I. N. Veeraswamy, Bombay . . .

The Langham Hotel's register had been brought to Detective-Sergeant Verney in the manager's office. He gazed at the names in despair. Did he really have to investigate the background of everyone with a room facing Broadcasting House? Suddenly he remembered. He had been ticked off last time for not searching promptly for the weapon. He must search all the fourth and fifth floor rooms on that side of the building at once.

"Surely that won't be necessary," protested the manager.

Verney prepared to be firm. Justice must be done, at whatever cost to the Langham Hotel's reputation.

"But it is a waste of time to search all these rooms," the manager objected. "If a guest of ours intended to shoot someone across the road in Broadcasting House, he would have to ask us for a room looking out in the right direction. I shall ask the receptionist at once, if such a thing occurred he will know."

After a very few minutes he was back. "As I thought, sergeant. Room 457, double with private bath, right on the corner which faces Broadcasting House. A Mrs Johnson, she asked for it specially. Booked in advance for last night and tonight."

"Oh good. Can I have a look at it?"

"Certainly, I will fetch a pass key."

Mrs Johnson, if that was her real name, had not made herself at home in room 457. A sparse collection of her toilet things was on the dressing table, but there were no clothes in the wardrobe or chest of drawers. A large cabin trunk stood in a corner, but it was locked. After an unsuccessful attempt which made his knuckles bleed, Verney managed to force the lock, but it contained only a large pile of telephone directories and some violently worded pamphlets about Ireland. Verney hid these away hastily in his brief case before the manager could see them. Nobody was allowed to know that the case had anything to do with Ireland.

"No doubt the trunk was used to smuggle the gun into the hotel," said the manager.

Verney crossed to the window. The light was still on in Chatham's office. He could see the scene quite distinctly. The photographer and the police surgeon and the fingerprint people were falling over each other in the limited space.

A description of Mrs Johnson, that was the next thing, and he had been taught all about getting descriptions of people at Hendon. The receptionist remembered her clearly. She had checked in at about nine the previous night, having called a week earlier to book the room. "Grey hair and a fresh face, one of those cheerful ladies with a loud voice. I think she'd have slapped me on the back if I hadn't been behind the desk."

"The Roedean type," said Verney.

"Beg pardon?"

"Nothing. What about her clothes?"

"The untidy country lady style, brown tweed not fitting properly, a great woollen scarf and a pork pie hat. A big heavy lady she was."

"Could it have been a man in disguise?"

The receptionist suppressed a snigger. "Funny sort of man . . . Come to think of it though, there was something odd about her."

"Was the grey hair a wig?"

"Difficult to tell, because of the hat. It was her face, I think. It wasn't big enough for the rest of her."

"Did she tell you why she wanted that particular room?"

"She said she was an artist and wanted a room she could sketch the church from. I thought it was a bit odd at the time."

It was a credible story. All Souls, Langham Place, with its round Doric porch crowned by a steeple, was a favourite London landmark and almost on the doorstep of Broadcasting House.

77

"I showed her several rooms," the receptionist went on, "and she chose that one because it had a bathroom."

Verney nodded. "To lock herself into if the maid came into the room."

"She wouldn't have to sit in there all day, sergeant," said the manager. "She'd walk out after breakfast with the key—it's missing, by the way—and hand it over to whoever did the shooting. That's assuming she didn't do it herself."

Verney's jaw dropped. "You mean, anyone could collect the key from her, go up to the room, take the gun out of the cabin trunk, fire the shot, and walk out of the hotel again without being challenged?"

"It's possible, yes, at most times of day."

"Even carrying a gun?"

"That would not strike the staff as odd, if it was in a gun-case. We have many guests travelling to and from Scotland and so on during the shooting season. I've had the bill made out for room 457 in case it tells us anything. Apart from bed and breakfast the only charge is for a local telephone call. The chit is in the handwriting of a switchboard operator who came on at four this afternoon."

"Did she note the number?" asked Verney eagerly.

"Welbeck 4468."

"I'll have it traced."

"I think you'll find it's the Broadcasting House number," said the manager.

Unaware that the citadel of British broadcasting had been under sniper fire, Helen Thackeray was spending the evening at home, working on the script of a discussion programme on the eighteenth-century novel which she was due to put on the air next day. Intending to have no truck with unscripted babble she had assembled the speakers in advance and recorded their rambling remarks on the blattnerphone, had them transcribed, and edited the result till it had clarity and shape. Tomorrow they would be handed their scripts to read. She began marking in the pauses, stresses and changes of tone which she would coach them into

78

reproducing at the microphone. Peter Warren complained that her discussion programmes sounded more like oratorios.

The doorbell rang. Chatham was outside, looking utterly distracted and miserable.

"Tony! Good gracious me, what's happened?"

"I drove straight here from Fontbury. Angela's starting divorce proceedings. I'm really on the skids this time."

Helen put aside her discussion script and resigned herself to dispensing consolation. She was fond of Tony and admired his work. It would be a disaster if he was hounded out of the BBC because of the neurotic behaviour of his silly wife. But she was getting very tired of these endless discussions of the Chatham marriage, and could not think of anything new to say about it.

"Tell me," she said nevertheless, pouring him a whisky.

"I hit her. The doctor's there, so that he can give evidence about her bruises. She's sent for her brother and the lawyer. She can divorce me for cruelty now."

Helen surreptitiously made his whisky a double. This was indeed a catastrophe. The BBC strained at the gnat of adultery. Cruelty was far too big a camel for it to swallow.

"She set out deliberately to make me lose my temper, I realise that now," Chatham went on. "Accusing me of starting an affair with my new secretary, and screaming in front of the servants that she was leaving me, and putting things in her luggage that had been in the house for generations and saying they were hers. I kept telling myself 'Stop it, she wants you to do this, she's trying for evidence of cruelty'. But I couldn't stop hitting her."

Helen was deeply distressed. He was intelligent, good with staff, full of programme flair. But in private life he was far too decent and defenceless to make a success of a marriage that was doomed from the start. Angela was an appalling snob. She had hawked herself around the county set in Wiltshire until the son and heir of a ducal house proposed marriage. But he had seen the danger signals in time and when he broke it off Chatham had caught her on the rebound. Why he wanted her goodness knows, no doubt it was one of those goatish urges that mysteriously afflict even the nicest men. When she let him see that he was only a substitute he cringed and

79

spoilt her to make up for the disappointment. He should have put her over his knee and spanked her years ago, but it was madness to have done so now.

What was Helen to say to him? Privately she was convinced that Peter Warren was at the root of the trouble. He was quite capable of having an affair with Angela out of spite, and egging her on to make Chatham's life a misery. But it was only a suspicion. If she hinted at it to Chatham, would that make matters better or worse?

While she was hesitating over this she noticed the time.

"The news," she said firmly, and switched on the radio. To listen to the main evening bulletin was part of the professional routine for senior staff.

The lead story was about a march by Sir Oswald Mosley's fascists in Bermondsey, with many injuries and arrests. Then came items about Japan's successful advance into China and some soothing words from Hitler's ambassador in Paris about his desire for friendly relations with the western democracies.

Halfway down the bulletin there was a short report of the shooting affair at Broadcasting House.

At Fontbury Angela Chatham was also listening to the news, while holding cold compresses to the bruises on her face and neck.

"Serve that ghastly old crocodile right," she commented on hearing that Lavinia Mannerton was dead. "She was the world's most avid mantrap, you could hear her wailing for demon lovers a mile away."

"She used to be a stunner, Angie," said her brother. "At those debs' dances you couldn't get near her for men."

"My dear Gerald, she looks like Elizabeth the First in extreme old age now. All that debauchery at Proctor's and the Silver Slipper, I suppose. I scarcely recognised her when I saw her in Tony's office."

"They seem to think she was shot in mistake for Tony."

"Why? She was very shootable in her own right, generations of injured wives must have been queueing up to extinguish her. Thank goodness I have an alibi."

"Good Lord, Tony wasn't having a thing with her as well as all the others, was he?"

"I doubt it, he doesn't like his gorgonzola as ripe as that. But I could easily have done it as an impersonal gesture of disapproval. Ouch, this eye of mine really hurts."

Gerald stood up and clenched his fists melodramatically. "I shan't rest till that caddish bully has his deserts."

"Well, it won't be long now," she said, wielding a hand mirror. "I'm glad you brought the camera, I'm beginning to look like the boxer who shouldn't have tried to make a come-back."

"I say, Angie. If you're divorcing him for cruelty, shouldn't you put back all that silver and stuff you've got in your trunks?"

"Should I? Why?"

"Because if he can say you've been stripping his house of heirlooms he can plead provocation for hitting you."

"Oh, very well, if you think so." She removed the cold compress from her eye. "This is coming along nicely. We'll photograph it again tomorrow. You can get colour films nowadays. Shall we try?"

"Excuse me, Miss, you're Mr Chatham's secretary, I believe?"

"I'm sorry, I can't talk to the press," said Jennifer, quickening her pace.

She had been under siege all morning, despite attempts by the switchboard girls to filter the calls to Chatham's extension. He was still busy with the police, and she had taken the brunt of press curiosity. As the finder of the body she was almost as much in demand as he was.

"I'm not a reporter, Miss," said the young man, hurrying along beside her.

She saw no reason to believe this. To avoid such encounters she would have preferred not to venture out of Broadcasting House, but the lunch hour was her only shopping time. All her stockings had laddered—she could only afford artificial silk. Decency required that they should be replaced.

"Anyway I don't know you," she said.

"Perhaps you've seen me around, Miss," said George Otway hopefully. "I used to work at the BBC."

Jennifer looked. The dark, heavily greased hair and the muscles bulging under an ill-fitting suit did seem vaguely familiar.

"What d'you want, anyway?"

"I was hoping," said George, "that you'd do me a favour and tell me Mr Peter Warren's home address."

"I can't possibly do that," said Jennifer.

She was walking faster and faster. He had to have the address. The letter he had sent to Warren at 5 Princess of Wales Avenue had been returned marked "Not known."

"Please, Miss. It's very important."

"Why d'you want it?"

"I'd like to send him a letter."

"You can send it to him at the BBC."

"It's personal, Miss. If I sent it there it might get opened."

She had to admit that this was only too true. Quite intimate personal mail had been known to end up in Programme Correspondence Unit.

"Please, Miss. I'm unemployed."

Jennifer softened a little. "I'll tell you what I'll do. Give me the letter and I'll hand it to Mr Warren myself."

"Oh thank you, Miss. Can I bring it tomorrow?"

"I . . . don't see why not."

"If I ring you, can you come down to reception and take it?"

"Very well. But I must go now, I have to do my shopping and get back to the office."

George Otway hurried back to his digs, well satisfied. If Warren would not talk to him, he could be written to.

There had been no word from the Director-General's office apart from a formal acknowledgement and a veiled hint that his appeal against his dismissal would be turned down if he talked to the press. He had little faith in the result, and judging from what they said at the Labour Exchange about other jobs, long term unemployment stared him in the face.

Warren must get him his job back. Otherwise he would raise one hell of a stink about Annie's death. It would serve him right. No fate was too bad for the man who had got Annie pregnant, then walked away and let her end up as a disgraced, dishevelled corpse on Wimbledon Common.

Burton fitted Lavinia's key into her front door, noting with approval the nice solid mortice lock. The flat was on the third floor of a walk-up block at the unprosperous end of the Fulham Road. The stairs and passages were uncarpeted and smelt of cats.

"I say, what a funny place for an earl's granddaughter to live," Verney exclaimed.

Burton gritted his teeth. Verney could not help being a half-baked public schoolboy with an accent that grated on his ear like a knife scraped on a plate. But by the same token Burton could not help hating Verney's guts. The super had told him to stop being so bloody uncooperative, and he was doing his best. It was easier not to be rude if he confined himself to monosyllables.

"Spy hole," he said, pointing to the one in the front door of the flat. The door opened into a lobby with a bathroom and a small kitchen off it. The door at the other end of the lobby was locked.

"I say, this one's got a spy hole too," said Verney. "It's like a medieval castle, isn't it? When the outer bastion fell, you withdrew into the keep."

Burton grunted and fitted another key from Lavinia's bunch into the inner door. It opened into the only room of the flat, which was comfortless and smelt of unemptied ashtrays. The furnishings were cheap and few. Nothing was in sight to reveal that the occupant was a woman. An alcove held a divan. Too many books were crammed into too few bookshelves.

Burton wandered round the room, opening drawers and cupboards at random. The bedside drawer contained a heavy service revolver. It was fully loaded.

"Smith and Wesson. Point four five," he remarked. "Funny set-up. All these locks and spy holes."

"I know. I wonder what she was afraid of?" said Verney.

Burton, with his corruptly acquired knowledge of Lavinia's past, could think of several answers which he was not in a position to mention. "You go through the chest of drawers, I'll take the desk," he said. Perhaps Lavinia's desk would yield a pretext for "remembering" a thing or two without having to give embarrassing explanations.

Though this hope was to be disappointed, he found going through the desk an absorbing task. Until he had finished he did not notice what Verney was doing, namely sitting in an armchair reading one of Lavinia's books.

"This is very interesting," said Verney, looking up.

"Is it now? Forgotten, have you? We've work to do."

"But this is work. Almost all her books are political. Very left wing."

"Subversive?"

"Marx and Engels and a lot about the Spanish Civil War."

"She gone communist then?"

"It doesn't follow. This one's by an anarchist as far as I can make out. He doesn't have a good word to say for the communists." He held the book out for inspection.

"*Homage to Catalonia* by George Orwell," Burton read. "He'll be on the other side then, with Franco and Mussolini and Hitler and all that."

"No, he doesn't seem keen on them either. According to him the Spanish communists have been shooting up the anarchists in Barcelona, but they both seem to be on the same side in the war. There are pamphlets and so on here from all sorts of left-wing groups. They seem to spend as much time arguing among themselves as they do fighting Franco. What did you find in her desk?"

"Cheque book," Burton reported. "Regular withdrawals every Thursday of fifty pounds in cash. That's a lot. She can't have spent it all on herself, not living in this dump." He opened the wardrobe. "Her clothes aren't up to much as far as I can see."

"You can spend a lot on drink," Verney suggested.

This was a possible explanation, from what Burton remembered. But the sideboard contained only a half-empty bottle of cheap sherry and another of gin. There were no empties in the cramped kitchen. Evidently Lavinia was a reformed character as far as alcohol went. On her past form drugs were also a possibility, but there had been no suggestion of that at the autopsy.

"Paying out to a blackmailer?" he suggested.

"Oh yes, that would explain it, wouldn't it? Was there anything else interesting in her desk?"

"Passport. She was in Spain for three months, from last November to early February this year. Correspondence, one or two letters in Spanish that I can't read, and quite a lot on politics."

"Who from?"

Burton consulted his notebook. "Someone called Philip Toynbee mostly. Two from a Stephen Spender and one from a Cecil Day Lewis."

"We'll have to find out about them. Are they pro-communist or pro-anarchist or what?"

"It's hard to tell really, they write in such an educated kind of way. There's a letter from her grandfather too—"

"Old Lord Ludgrove? Is he still alive?"

"He was a fortnight ago, anyway. He says how nice it was of her to come and see him and he's glad she's leading a more settled life what with her job at the BBC, and he encloses a cheque. No trace of cheque."

"Perhaps that's why she can afford to draw fifty pounds a week on her account," Verney suggested.

But what the hell does she spend it on, Burton thought as he looked round the forlorn room. Quite a change from the Silver Slipper days. But if she'd gone into left-wing politics that would explain it.

"Let's search the whole place properly now," he suggested. "You start in the bathroom, I'll take the kitchen."

Neither of them found anything meaningful.

"You check the cistern of the bog?" Burton asked.

"Oh. Actually no, I didn't."

"You should have. When they want to hide something they often think 'Ooh, that would be a good place, no one would think of looking there.' Let's see."

He stood on the seat of the WC and investigated. Apart from the flush mechanism there was nothing but water in the cistern, but taking off the lid had revealed a small piece of cardboard wedged in the crack between it and the wall. He reached up and pulled it out.

It was an empty Players' cigarette packet opened out flat, with writing on the inner side; a series of six-figure numbers. All but the last one were crossed through.

Six figures. Written with different pens and pencils, at different times. And whatever she had used to write the new figure had also been used to cross the previous one out. Well, obviously . . . he went back into the living room and looked round. There was only one picture, a horrible thing, all sharp angles in dingy greys and browns representing bits of a guitar that had been hacked to pieces and thrown on a rubbish dump. He took the picture down. The dial of a wall safe was revealed.

He handed the Players packet to Verney. "Read me out the last one, the one that isn't crossed out. If you change the setting regularly you have to write it down in case you forget."

"We're in luck, we'll probably find out what she did with the money," said Verney excitedly.

"Just read out the figures," Burton replied between set teeth, "and we'll see."

But the safe was empty.

TEN

HAROLD MILLBANK HAD decided that "Murdered BBC Secretary Aided Spanish Reds" would look well in a headline and be a disagreeable surprise for Sir John Reith. So far he only had it on the word of a neighbour in Lavinia's block of flats who clearly did not know her very well. But the paper had a contact who specialised in Spanish politics and followed the activities of Republican supporters in London. Millbank had summoned him post-haste.

"Lavinia Mannerton? I thought you knew, she was Alf Dunn's mistress, a very prestigious thing to be. He was one of the first British volunteers to join the International Brigade and go out there, oh a splendid chap, a hulking great unemployed miner from County Durham. He's quite famous."

"Never heard of him," said Millbank.

"You wouldn't have, it's the left-wing intellectuals and the eighteen-year-old communist poets from Eton who get the publicity when they go out to Spain. They're only a handful; the bulk of the British contingent comes from the politically conscious working class, chaps like Alf Dunn."

"Where on earth," Millbank asked, "did Lavinia Mannerton pick up a beefy unemployed miner from County Durham?"

"In London, I suppose. Those early volunteers were around here for a bit while they were organising themselves to get to Spain, it was before the volunteers' trail via the Gare d'Austerlitz got going properly. The left-wing intellectuals were all over them like bees round a honeypot, too thrilling, my dear, fancy meeting a real live member of the working class. Anyway, Dunn did well in Spain, turned out to be a natural leader and commanded a company in the University City battle, but he got killed on the Andujar front at the end of December and Lavinia Mannerton came home."

"He took her out there with him?"

87

"Not as a camp follower, she got herself a job as an orderly in one of the Madrid hospitals. She looked awful when she came back, having lost the love of her life, and the *Daily Worker* crowd gave her a bad time which didn't help."

"Oh, why was that?" asked Millbank, making a note.

"She'd let fall some rather tasteless remarks about her Alf having been deliberately sent to his death by the political commissar of the brigade, who of course was a proper Moscow-trained communist, and as one knows those people do have instructions to weed out non-communists who are making friends and influencing people."

"So Alf Dunn wasn't a communist?"

"No, I think you'd class him as a self-taught anarchist, though that's a silly name for what the POUM anarchists believe in. The Moscow-based faithful hate them like poison, they had quite a lot of them shot as Franco spies. As for them doing in Alf Dunn, there may be nothing in it but she insisted that there was."

"And that made her unpopular with King Street when she got back?"

"Oh yes, they reacted with a nasty little whispering campaign. I don't remember the details. Something about her embezzling money out of some fighting fund."

"Ah," said Millbank. "Can you find out a bit more about that?"

"I'll try. But do remember, these people will say anything about each other that seems convenient, however nasty and far-fetched; provided, of course, that the outside world goes on thinking they're all standing shoulder to shoulder in defence of a noble ideal."

"Rather like the BBC," said Millbank.

Chatham had arrived for the day's work to find one of Miss Proctor's hennaed battleaxes in possession of the secretary's desk. He had encountered her before. Violet something . . .

"Hullo, Violet. What's happened to Jennifer?"

"Miss Proctor sent her back to General Office."

"Oh, why?"

"The press kept asking to speak to her. She's not at all discreet. Miss Proctor says she's been talking out of turn."

"What nonsense. The press have been on to this office from dawn till dusk for a week, she didn't slip up once."

"Miss Proctor says she made up a lot of nonsense to tell the police, to make herself seem important."

"It sounds very unlike Jennifer, but I'll talk to Miss Proctor about it later. Any messages?"

There were several, but before Violet could give him the details she had to answer the telephone. "Miss Howe doesn't work here anymore. Can I do anything for you? . . . Oh, it's personal, is it? No, I've no idea where you can reach her. . . . No, I'm sorry, I really can't help you."

She slammed down the receiver on its hook and turned to Chatham.

"A young man for your Jennifer," she sneered acidly, as if that proved Miss Proctor's point.

"Why didn't you tell him where she was?"

"We can't have them taking personal calls in the typing pool."

Outside a phone box in Oxford Circus underground station, George Otway twisted his carefully composed letter to Peter Warren between his fingers and wondered what to do next.

Chatham, meanwhile, was making an internal telephone call. "Good morning, Commodore."

"Good morning, Tony. What can I do for you?"

"Could we cancel the special car and the security men?"

"Hm. I don't like it."

"Nothing's been happening. My madman's probably so shocked at shooting the wrong person that he's decided to call the whole thing off."

"We can't be sure of that."

"I'm willing to take the risk."

"No doubt. But if you're gunned down in Portland Place I shall be the inept callous bureaucrat that let it happen."

"You could tell the press I insisted. The point is, I feel such a heel, skulking about behind a security screen when that totally innocent woman ought to be alive and I ought to be dead."

This was language which the Commodore understood and found hard to resist. "You're sure? I still don't like it."

89

"Quite sure. I'll go mad if I have to lurk in that Dolphin Square hide-out any longer."

"Right, I'll call the whole thing off," said the Commodore reluctantly. One couldn't keep protecting a chap against his will . . .

The Commodore was not happy about the turn the police investigation was taking. Because of something they had been told by a temporary secretary in Chatham's office, a flighty unreliable girl by all accounts, they believed that the marksman in the Langham Hotel had made no mistake: Lavinia Mannerton had always been the intended victim and the shenanigans aimed at Chatham had been nothing more than an elaborate blind.

This would not have mattered if Miss Mannerton had not turned out to have a past so lurid as to raise the question why on earth the BBC was employing her. Luckily nothing had appeared in the press yet, apart from a vague hint or two. Sir Stephen Tallents, who looked after the BBC's press relations, was on excellent terms with the Fleet Street proprietors. Miss Mannerton was an earl's granddaughter, and all concerned agreed that publicising the moral turpitude of the upper classes was grist to the Left's political mill and should be avoided as far as possible. But if the press got wind of the suggestion that Miss Mannerton was the intended victim, her background would become a matter of public interest and nothing would hold back the flood of adverse publicity for the BBC.

With any luck this awkward police theory would prove wrong. Meanwhile, all the BBC could do was to go on hiding behind the threatening letters which no one was allowed to see from an Irishman who did not exist. He made a note to ring the Commissioner of Police and persuade him to hold the position a little longer. After that he would give that clown Warren a dressing down for bringing the wretched Mannerton woman into the BBC.

It would have been better from every point of view, he thought, if he could have gone on surrounding Chatham with anxious precautions for his safety.

*

Millbank's Spanish specialist lost no time in finding out why Lavinia Mannerton was being accused of financial irregularities.

"It wasn't a fighting fund, Harold," he reported. "It was what you might call ex-servicemen's relief. Chaps who've been wounded or had a bellyful of the fighting come back from Spain and can't get jobs, and their insurance isn't paid up so they can't claim unemployment benefit, and the Government's attitude is serve them right for going to Spain where they'd no business to be. Lavinia Mannerton was doling out weekly postal orders to over a dozen of them to keep them going."

"I don't see anything wrong with that," said Millbank.

"Ah but you see, she was choosy. Anarchists and ordinary decent chaps were in, anyone tainted with the Moscow tarbrush was out, because they had allegedly killed her lover. And of course this provoked frightful rumblings of thunder from King Street. What is this effete member of the oppressive landowning class up to? Who is she to decide that some should be helped and others not? Why is money subscribed for the cause not available to all on a democratic basis? How did this class enemy get her hands on it?"

"Where *does* the money come from?" asked Millbank.

"Goodness knows, she's been living on nothing a week like a grim left-wing nun. Could she be saving it out of a private income?"

"My sources say she doesn't have one."

"Well, some very odd things have happened to funds subscribed by the public for Spain. I suppose there could be something in what the Kremlin spokesmen say. By the way, I've brought something to show you, take a look at this."

Diving into his brief case he produced a badly printed photograph of a very handsome young man with wavy fair hair, posed in a heroic attitude against a stormy sky. It formed the front of a pamphlet containing jaunty verses of left-wing inspiration.

"*Poems of Revolution*," Millbank read. "By—my God, is he any relation?"

"*Poems of Revolution* by Michael Chatham. Yes, he's your Chatham's nephew, the son of the elder brother. Or was, rather; he was killed in Spain. Your Chatham keeps very quiet about him for fear of besmirching the BBC."

"Good looking," said Millbank.

"Yes, that was why they chose him, he was all set to become a sort of Marxist matinée idol. Then suddenly a sort of mystery developed, his picture wasn't being splashed around anymore."

"Why? What happened?"

"Nobody knows, but about a fortnight after he was killed King Street began to throw out hints that Chatham-worship wasn't exactly party-line."

"Oh goody goody. I want to know a lot more about this," said Millbank.

"Bailey may know something."

Bailey was the paper's correspondent in Madrid.

Millbank lifted the telephone. "Book me a call to the Gran Via hotel in Madrid. Personal, for John Bailey."

"You'll be lucky," said the operator.

But the call did come through. In time for the country edition, too.

"Red Spain and the BBC, a mysterious link," Helen Thackeray read. "How disgusting."

She handed the newspaper back to Chatham by one corner, as if she had found someone else's dirty handkerchief.

"Millbank is a very disgusting man," said Chatham. "Most of what he says is true, though. It's the way it's put."

"You mean, you did go to Madrid last winter?"

"Yes."

"And pretended you were going skiing in Switzerland, as he says? Yes, I remember you talking about it."

"I was afraid Reith would try to stop me for fear of adverse publicity. But there's no real secret about why I went. It was to get Michael home."

"Could you have, if he hadn't been killed?"

"The Romillys got their boy back."

"Only because he wanted to marry that girl. Besides, he was under age. Michael was twenty-two."

"I know, but I had to try. Otherwise I'd never have been able to look myself in the face again. Don't you see? My father had just died, Fontbury had passed to Michael because his father who was killed at Passchendaele was my elder brother. How could I sit in London and wait to inherit Fontbury as soon as Michael was shot by some fascist sniper?"

Helen glanced at the newspaper. "It says here that he was killed a week before you arrived . . ."

"Quite true, but you've no idea of the utter chaos. There are no proper army records. Letters don't get through, deaths aren't notified. It was ages before I found anyone who knew anything about him, and longer before I found out he was dead."

"Millbank seems to be hinting that there was some mystery about Michael. He says all the publicity about him stopped soon after he was killed."

There was a silence. Chatham's defences had gone up. He was wearing what she thought of as his parade ground face.

"Helen, if I tell you something, will you promise never to repeat it to anyone?"

"Of course, Tony."

"Michael wasn't killed in the University City battle. He was shot as a fascist spy."

"*Michael* was? Surely that's absurd?"

"Of course it is, no one who knew him could credit it for a moment."

"Who says so?"

"I was told by a boy called John Cornford, rather a good communist poet, much better than Michael. He was killed a few weeks later, on his twenty-first birthday."

"Was he telling the truth?"

"I think so. I had to drag the story out of him. He hated admitting that communism ever made a mistake."

"But was he there when it happened?"

"No, Michael was in the Thaelmann battalion and Cornford wasn't, he had it at second-hand from Esmond Romilly, who was. But if it's not true, why did the build-up of Michael as a sort of Marxist Horst Wessel suddenly stop?"

"It seems so unlikely," Helen protested.

"Anything's possible in that atmosphere. There was a lot of

spy-fever in Madrid just then, they'd caught several genuine Franco spies. According to Cornford there'd been rumours that one of the Britons in the Thaelmann battalion was related to a prominent Conservative politician. It was Esmond Romilly of course, he's a nephew of that windbag Winston Churchill. But they didn't know that, and when Michael was caught trying to contact the British Embassy they got very suspicious—"

"But surely the Embassy took refuge in Hendaye quite early in the war?"

"There's a skeleton staff still in Madrid to rescue disillusioned heroes who want to come home, in fact they do discreetly encourage desertions. So from the orthodox communist point of view they're afflicted with leprosy."

"Why was Michael getting in touch with them?"

"I asked them that. They said they'd had no contact with him, which was probably true."

After a long silence Helen said: "My poor Tony."

"D'you see now why I hate the thought of being divorced and having to live at Fontbury and play the country squire? I'd be stepping into the shoes of a boy who had the guts to get killed for a cause he thought worth fighting for."

"But his cause was flawed."

"That doesn't make any difference. All causes are flawed to some extent."

"Yours isn't. Somehow you must get Angela to change her mind."

"Are you sure the BBC isn't flawed?" said Chatham.

When the superintendent summoned Verney and Burton to his office at Vine Street to report progress, a tall grim-faced Scot was with him.

"Come in, you two," said the superintendent. "This is a murder case now, and there's a lot of public interest. From now on you'll be reporting to Inspector Galbraith here."

Burton cursed inwardly, but not because a senior detective from Scotland Yard had been brought in over his and Verney's heads to take any credit that was going. He had expected that, and was hoping for someone tactful enough to listen to his revelations about Lavinia Mannerton's past without asking how he had come by them. But Galbraith, Goddard's successor as station sergeant at Vine Street! He was a strait-laced puritanical bastard, who had done his best to shop Burton as well as Goddard when the scandal broke. There could be no question of confiding in him.

Galbraith was leafing through Verney's elegantly worded report, which had cost him a lot of trouble. "Nae doubt ye will learn in time," he told the proud author, "tae express yourself more concisely. Ye say here, Warren denies having made a telephone call tae Broadcasting House on the afternoon of Miss Mannerton's murder."

"Yes, Inspector," said Verney eagerly. "And of course he was on his way from Royal Lodge to Oxford at the time, and anyway we know that the call came from the Langham Hotel."

Galbraith threw him what might easily be taken for a look of loathing, and turned a page of his report.

"The BBC seem to think we're paying too much attention to that phone call," Verney went on. "They say the secretary who overheard it isn't a reliable witness."

"We willna attach importance tae what they say," replied Galbraith severely.

The superintendent nodded agreement. "The BBC rolls itself up like a damn hedgehog whenever anything awkward happens."

"That Miss Howe seemed very level-headed to me," said Burton.

Galbraith went on reading Verney's report. "This wall safe, now. Have ye no clue tae what use she made of it?"

"To keep money in, if you ask me," said Burton. "She'd been paying quite large sums into her account in cash."

"Constable Burton went to her bank this morning," Verney put in helpfully.

"When ye say large sums, Burton," Galbraith persisted, "tae what order of magnitude do ye refer?"

"Several hundred pounds at a time."

Galbraith stared at him meaningfully. "And ye say ye found the safe empty?"

Burton returned the stare, then turned to Verney. "I didn't notice any money in it, did you, sergeant?"

"Er, no. It was empty, I'm quite sure," said Verney with no idea what all this was about.

You bastard, thought Burton, glaring at Galbraith. As though any policeman in his senses would pocket cash from a murder victim's safe with a virgin-faced tightarse like Verney looking on. It was Galbraith's way of reminding him that the Goddard business was not forgotten.

"And what did ye discover at the bank?" Galbraith asked.

"Once or twice a month she'd pay in two or three hundred, perhaps more, in notes. There was no regular pattern. But every Thursday in her lunch hour, regular as clockwork, she drew out fifty pounds which she took across the road and bought money orders with it. Then she put the money orders into ready-addressed envelopes that she'd brought with her, and posted them."

"Do we know who to?"

"Yes, Inspector. Volunteers who came back from Spain, wounded and so on. From what one hears, they need it."

"Has she travelled abroad at all, since she returned frae Spain?"

"Not according to her passport," said Verney. "But the BBC say she was away for a long weekend just before she was killed."

"Went to see her grandfather in Cheshire," Burton added. "Hoping for a sub for her relief fund, no doubt. He sent her a cheque for ten quid."

"The report from ballistics has just come in," said the superintendent, producing it. "The bullet that wounded Chatham came from the same gun as the one that killed Miss Mannerton. It's an unusual calibre, point four seven five, they think it was probably a sporting rifle, a Mannlicher or something like that. But about the third bullet—"

"And which one would that be?" Galbraith interrupted.

"When Chatham was driving away from here in a cab," the superintendent explained, "he was fired at a second time from a moving car. They missed."

"It wouldna be convenient tae fire a rifle from a moving

vehicle," Galbraith remarked. "Some smaller weapon, nae doubt."

"It was a point four five," said the superintendent. "Probably a Smith and Wesson revolver, they say. But they admit it's only a guess. Any other developments to report?"

"Only that Chatham's asked for the security precautions to be lifted," said Verney. "He's moving back to his own flat in Imperial Court."

The superintendent nodded. "It's obvious that shooting at him was a blind, to make us concentrate on his background and not Miss Mannerton's."

"Which we'd ha' done," Galbraith added, "if the lassie hadna overheard that telephone conversation."

PART TWO

In which the Guilty watch
Police Activity in growing
Alarm

ELEVEN

"A CURSE ON eavesdropping little Jennifer," said Peter Warren, striding anxiously up and down the room. "She's put us in a very tricky position."

"Do sit down, Peter," Angela begged. "Marching about and knocking over the furniture won't make it any less tricky."

"I'm sure we'll be all right if we keep our heads," Chatham reasoned, in the reassuring tone he used to soothe ruffled feelings at meetings.

They had travelled separately to a weekend cottage near Marlow, whose absentee owner thought Peter Warren had borrowed it for purposes connected with his unremitting love-life. It was deep in a wood. Neither the lights from the windows nor the three cars parked beside it could be seen from the lane. The three of them had held planning sessions there ever since they decided that Lavinia Mannerton's blackmailing activities would have to stop. It was here that they had settled the details of Operation Lavinia and rehearsed the fierce quarrels they intended to wage in front of witnesses, for the whole thing hinged on no one suspecting that three people who seemed to be barely on speaking terms could have conspired to manufacture a watertight alibi.

"Thanks to eavesdropping little Jennifer," Warren went on, "our mad Irish assassin is no more. The curse is come upon us, damn it, as the Lady of Shalott remarked."

"All is not yet lost," said Angela. "Don't float down to Camelot in a boat till you have to."

"I do think you're being over-anxious, Peter," said Chatham. "It's a pity about the Irishman, but they can't prove anything if we sit tight. In military terms, our outposts have been overrun but our main defensive position remains intact."

"Yes, but there is one slight problem," Angela objected. "Our main defensive position consists of the three of us screaming and scratching at each other like three cats in a bag, so that no one suspects Peter and me of giving you an alibi for the shooting. . . . Thanks to eavesdropping little Jennifer, we'll have to go on screaming and scratching indefinitely."

"Oh no, Angie. A little longer than we expected, that's all."

"A lot longer," she insisted. "We were going to drop it as soon as the police got tired of looking for a non-existent Irishman. They know now that the Irishman's a figment, they're asking themselves who had a motive for extinguishing that public inconvenience Lavinia Mannerton. They'll be sniffing around for ages, and I can't go on forever threatening to divorce you and not doing it."

"We may have to think in terms of a discreet clinic in Switzerland," said Chatham. "You needn't actually go there, of course. You could hide out in Monte Carlo or somewhere under another name."

"Oh Tony, you darling beast, what can you mean?"

"The difficulty over divorce would be solved if you switched to an all-out nervous breakdown."

She considered this. "It's happened before in a sensational murder case. But I don't see myself moaning on the stairs with a candle, I'm not the Lady Macbeth type."

Warren knocked over his chair as he stood up. "Stop being so damn flippant, it turns me up."

Angela threw Chatham an enquiring look. He nodded. Warren would be easier to handle without her there.

"Well, I shall start making scrambled eggs and coffee," she announced, and moved off to the kitchen.

Chatham watched her go with a little thrill of excitement. The transformation was amazing. A year ago she had scarcely been conscious of his existence, except as the man she had happened to marry in the black moment of despair after her engagement to Bill Stockbridge was broken off. Later when Chatham inherited Fontbury she had started to take notice of him because it gave her landed gentry status, but the faint frown of dissatisfaction stayed. Bill Stockbridge was the Duke of Andover's heir.

It was Operation Lavinia that had done the trick. He had started down the road of crime for her sake. She knew it and the knowledge excited her. So did the planning; she proved to have a zestful capacity for detail and some of her suggestions were brilliant. The change in her attitude was astonishing, out of bed as well as in. She saw him with new eyes. It was as if Bill Stockbridge had never existed.

When she had gone Peter Warren plumped down into a too-small fireside chair which gave a loud crack under his weight. "God, why did I get into this?"

"Because you didn't enjoy being blackmailed by Lavinia anymore than I did," said Chatham. "She was getting very greedy."

"My God," Warren repeated, rubbing his knuckles in a fever of anxiety.

This would need handling carefully, Chatham decided, but he was not really worried yet. Warren had been at school with him, he could read him like a book. For instance, his misery at being blackmailed by Lavinia had showed at once, getting the truth out of him had been child's play. As fellow-victims of Lavinia's they were in the same boat, and in one respect Warren was an ideal accomplice. He was a first-class shot, an ideal person to have on the other end of the gun if one proposed to stand on a kerb with one's arm in the air waiting for it to be shot at in order to make sure the police went off on the wrong track.

But Warren had his limitations. He had no real grasp of detail and veered far too sharply between overmastering confidence and jittering nerves. Look at him now. He must be reassured, but not too much. Warren the master criminal would be a worse danger to all three of them than Warren in a blind panic.

Fortunately, Chatham had been able even at school to manipulate Warren without Warren realising what was happening. Indeed, it was at school that he had made a useful discovery. Nature had endowed him with the sort of face, voice and temperament which enabled him to give an appearance of sympathetic apprecia-tion of the other person's viewpoint, then get his own way without appearing to be cleverer or more forceful than anyone else. He had pulled the trick off so often at BBC meetings that it was no longer a conscious technique.

"I do see why you're worried, Peter," he began. "But I think, don't you, that all will be well if we're careful. We did discuss this possibility, you know, we knew there was a risk of that phone call being overheard and we planned for it. It's a nuisance, but I don't think it's a disaster."

"It is for me, damn it. Who else but me would have rung Lavinia and asked her to rifle your desk? They must have guessed it was me."

"But Peter, they know you were in Oxford. Why would they suspect that you rang from there? Remember, they know that a call to Broadcasting House was charged to room 457 at the Langham Hotel that afternoon."

"Do they?" asked Warren, biting his nails savagely.

"Surely you remember? We checked."

The idea of the duplicate phone calls had been one of Angela's ingenious touches of detail. While Warren talked to Lavinia from a phone box in Oxford Chatham had made a call from room 457 at the Langham Hotel to a Broadcasting House extension that he knew was unmanned. They had made sure in advance that the Langham switchboard noted down the numbers of local calls. Angela had persuaded an aunt to stay there and devised an unobtrusive way of checking.

"Oh my God," Warren repeated gloomily.

Chatham was puzzled. Warren's sex habits had got him into tight corners before, but in the end he had always managed to pull himself together and keep his head. During the planning of Operation Lavinia he had joined quite calmly in the discussion of things that might go wrong and what would have to be done about them. This utter collapse was unlike him.

For a moment their eyes met, and what Chatham saw gave him a clue. "Peter, there's something you haven't told me."

Warren nodded miserably. "I've been meaning to all evening, but I funked it."

When it came down to rock bottom, Warren was afraid of him. That was the central feature of their relationship.

"Out with it, Peter."

"Oh God, you know that damn Vasco da Gama feature that I made such a muck of?"

"Yes, I wondered about that. Music Department's balance and control people are quite competent really."

"No, it was my fault. One of them looked a bit familiar, and halfway through the broadcast I realised that it was Anne Otway's brother."

Chatham thought carefully. "Did he recognise you?"

"He's always known my name."

"What else does he know?"

"Only that I had an affair with Anne and paid for the abortion."

"So he doesn't know that Lavinia was acting as a tout for that grossly incompetent Harley Street abortionist?"

"No."

"Nor that Lavinia helped you to get Anne into the car so that you could dump her on Wimbledon Common?"

"No."

"Nor that the bloody fingerprints they found on Anne's patent leather handbag were yours and not the abortionist's?"

"No."

"In that case it's just an unfortunate coincidence and I don't see the worry. Otway doesn't know that Lavinia comes into the picture and won't suspect that she was blackmailing you."

"I haven't told you the whole story yet," said Warren in a gulp. "You see, there wasn't time to talk it over with you and it seemed a good idea . . ."

"What did, Peter?"

"Getting him the sack." The story came out in a miserable rush; how he had followed Otway and the rest of the balance and control team into the Stag's Head without having decided what, if anything, he would say to Otway; how Otway had gone to the gents leaving his beer in an unobserved corner, the two double whiskies . . . "I had to make up my mind quick, I knew he'd be back in a minute."

"You know, you should have told me about this at once," said Chatham as calmly as he could.

"I know, but by then the whole thing had started. Angela had smuggled herself and the gun into the Langham, and anyway it didn't seem very dangerous then. I didn't think he'd realise it was me interfering with his beer."

"But he did?" asked Chatham, controlling his voice with an effort.

"Yes, but I only found out hours later. By then you'd driven the Delage to Battersea for me to collect and there was no way of getting hold of you."

"You could have phoned me in the room at the Langham."

"I suppose so. I didn't think of it."

"You mean, you were afraid I'd call the whole thing off and let Lavinia bleed you to death. Tell me exactly what happened." Never show anger, he told himself, never let people see the contempt you feel.

"This is awful, I know you'll be furious. Otway pounced on me as I came out of Broadcasting House and said I must get him his job back or else, and I brushed him off because there wasn't time to argue. If I got held up it would upset the alibi. But he followed me."

"How far?"

"All the way. To Battersea."

"You mean he saw you get the Delage out of the garage?"

"Yes. I'm sorry."

Somehow Chatham managed not to yell at him. This was an almighty upset, coming on top of Jennifer Howe's eavesdropping. But the important thing now was to keep Warren as calm as possible. He counted three, then said: "I daresay something can be done about young Otway."

"I thought a road accident?"

"Oh no, let's avoid being crude if possible. The BBC's definitely sacked him?"

"I think he's appealed to the DG, but the appeal hasn't been considered yet."

"Then one obvious step suggests itself."

"Oh. Yes, I see what you mean . . ."

Angela reappeared from the kitchen with a trayful of food.

"Would it make Peter happier," she suggested, "if we hinted in the right quarter that eavesdropping little Jennifer is a liar and didn't hear what she says she did?"

"That's already being attended to by the Corporation," Chatham told her.

"Good gracious, darling. The ways it moves in are more mysterious than God's."

"It's trying to shift public attention away from Lavinia by bringing our Irishman back to life."

"I'm sorry, I don't follow."

"Well, if the Irishman was trying to shoot me, it follows that Lavinia was shot by mistake. So there's no need to look too closely into her background and with any luck the press won't ask why the Corporation was employing a woman with her rather extraordinary past as a senior secretary. If Lavinia was shot by mistake, it follows that no one phoned her and told her to go into my office—in order to be shot. If no one phoned her then it follows that Jennifer, who says someone did, is a liar."

Angela frowned. "Then shouldn't you and Peter join in the chorus of denigration? 'Poor little thing, she was very highly strung and kept hearing voices like Joan of Arc'?"

"Hear, hear," said Peter. "Let's bring the Irishman back to life."

"I did consider that," said Chatham. "But it would be dangerous if we seemed to have a vested interest in him."

"But he could send another threatening letter. That wouldn't bring us into the picture."

"Except that his typewriter's in the Thames near Shepperton Lock," Angela put in.

"I honestly don't think this idea's worth pursuing, do you?" said Chatham. "I don't see how the attempt to resuscitate the Irishman can possibly succeed."

"It will if I have another shot at you," said Warren.

"Thank you. I don't think that will help."

"Why not? I did a damn good job, lots of blood and no permanent damage."

"Because it might make them more suspicious. So far the

Irishman's score is a bull's-eye on Lavinia and an outer and a miss on me. They know he can shoot properly when he tries, so why does he keep missing me?"

"I suppose you're right," Peter murmured, pushing away his half-eaten plateful with a suppressed belch of disgust.

Chatham watched the idea come to him: if I shoot Tony stone dead the Irishman will come to life with a vengeance. That train of thought had better be dealt with at once.

"Before I forget, Peter, I'd like the Luger back."

The Luger pistol was a wartime souvenir, taken off a dead German officer by Chatham's elder brother. Warren had used it to shoot a hole in Chatham's taxi window as he left Vine Street police station.

"It's in my car," said Warren.

"Would you fetch it, please, if you've finished eating?"

Warren went reluctantly.

"He's got the willies, Tony," said Angela. "Is he going to crack up?"

"I hope not. He's done something rather silly, I'll tell you later. While we're on the subject of guns, I've put the rifle in the boot of your car."

"Good. I'll drive over to Aunt Gertrude's with it tomorrow."

Angela's Great-Aunt Gertrude lived in Northamptonshire, in a house where horned beasts gazed down from the walls at tigerskin rugs with stuffed heads which snarled up at them from the floors. It had occurred to Chatham that the arsenal used by the late Great-Uncle Everard to effect this slaughter was probably still in the house. Moreover Aunt Gertrude was ninety and almost blind and her staff of three was tottering into its eighties, so that a sporting rifle borrowed from its gun room for a week or so was not likely to be missed. Investigation by Angela on the pretext of visiting the sick had shown that these assumptions were correct.

"I'll put it back tomorrow and take her some grapes as a thank you," she said.

Warren had come back with the Luger pistol. "What'll you do with it?"

"Put it where it won't be found," said Chatham.

"We ought to keep a gun of some kind handy," Warren protested.

"Yes, I thought so too," said Chatham, putting it in his brief case.

There was a moment of ugly tension. To defuse it Chatham produced a large manila envelope from his brief case and spilled the contents on to the table.

"From Lavinia's safe?" Warren asked.

Chatham nodded. He had emptied her safe on his way from the garage in Battersea to room 457 at the Langham Hotel, an operation made possible by careful planning. In an office emergencies occur or can be manufactured which force a secretary to leave her handbag unattended on her desk for long enough to take an impression of her doorkey. Annoyingly Lavinia had two, for an inner and an outer door. Filing down blanks to make duplicates that worked had taken weeks, but it was worth it. A quick visit to her flat while she was at work had led to the discovery of the safe. While Lavinia was on her begging visit to her grandfather Chatham had spent two days searching the flat for the note she must have made somewhere of the combination, for only people with enormous confidence in their memory for figures fail to write it down. Like Detective-Constable Burton, he did not neglect the WC cistern.

"Your stuff's here somewhere, Peter," he said, searching among the papers which littered the table. "Ah, this is it."

The collection relating to Warren was clipped together. The main item was a long press cutting from the *Wimbledon Gazette*, an account of the inquest on Anne Otway. Lavinia had underlined the paragraph in which the police gave evidence that the fingerprints on the dead girl's handbag had proved impossible to identify. Clipped to the press cutting were some enlarged photographs of a tumbler with powdered fingerprints on it. Warren's name and address were written on the back of each. Two more press cuttings dealt with the trial of a Harley Street practitioner of dubious qualifications on a charge which was primly described as "the use of an instrument".

Looking rather green, Warren put the cuttings aside. "Isn't there anything there about you?"

"There was," said Chatham, "but there isn't now."

"I still don't know what she had on you."

"No," said Chatham, outfacing him with a pleasant smile which was also a stare.

"But you know all about me."

"Well, yes. You were very distressed and confided in me. That's why we decided to tackle the thing together." Chatham picked up a battered penny notebook from the table. "Have a look at this."

The notebook was cash-ruled. At the head of each page was a name, with sums of money opposite dates below. Warren flipped over the pages. "Good Lord, we weren't the only milch-cows, were we? And half these people are in the BBC."

"Well, we expected that," said Chatham, suppressing a twinge of conscience, for he regretted the need to expose his colleagues to risk. It had been his suggestion that Warren should feign appeasement of his blackmailer and offer to get her into the BBC as his secretary. She had snapped up the bait greedily, knowing that Broadcasting House under Reith's puritanical eye contained the most blackmailable group of people in London.

"She must have felt like a fox being ushered into the hen-run by the farmer," said Angela.

Warren turned over the pages of the notebook and found Chatham's entry. "My God, she squeezed a lot out of you, more than me."

"I suppose she thought I was richer," said Chatham. He picked up papers at random from the table. "It's surprising what some of our colleagues got up to. I can't see *her* shoplifting, can you? . . . He worked for Radio Luxembourg on the side under another name, I thought Lavinia would get on to that, a lot of people knew . . . We all know about *him*, but who's Hotchkiss? Oh yes, the talks producer, I feel bad about that. There was a conviction for a homosexual offence that he managed to hush up, but Lavinia got on to him and he killed himself, the payments stop in August . . ."

But Warren was taking no interest.

"Cheer up, this is the best news yet," said Chatham. "They'll probably decide she was a blackmailer, but she's widened the field beautifully. With a fistful of suspected victims to choose from they'll never get round to us."

"Won't they?" asked Warren listlessly.

"No. We've got alibis."

TWELVE

"Look, sarge," said Detective-Constable Burton, "who else would have made that phone call? It must have been Warren."

"But my dear chap, he says he didn't," Verney objected, "and we know he was in Oxford."

"He could have phoned from Oxford."

"You mean to say, it was just a coincidence when she was shot a few minutes later?"

"No, sarge, you're not concentrating. He was someone else's accomplice. He and the sniper in the Langham had synchronised their watches."

"Oh I say, isn't that a bit far-fetched?"

"I look at it this way. She was a blackmailer, right?"

"That's only a guess."

"How else d'you explain all that money coming into her account in cash? Let's suppose two of her victims compare notes and discover she's milking them both. They'd join forces to do her in."

Verney shook his shoulders petulantly. "What would she be blackmailing Warren about?"

"Untidy sex habits. They're hot on that in the BBC."

Verney treated him to another amused shrug. Burton bit back the thing he dared not say: Don't look at me like that, you little fool, I know a compulsive fornicator when I see one, and I bet Warren's got more than one girl into trouble in his time. And what's more, when that Harley Street quack got done for procuring a very slipshod line in abortions, Goddard and I did nicely out of keeping Lavinia Mannerton's name out of court.

"I say, you do have a dirty mind," said Verney. "Who's Warren an accomplice of?"

Burton took a deep breath. "Chatham. She was blackmailing him over something that happened in Spain."

"Oh really, old man—"

"Listen. I've been talking to that fellow Millbank—"

"Oh, but Inspector Galbraith told us to leave talking to the press to him."

"We'd never get anywhere, would we, if we always did what the inspector says? Millbank has informers in the BBC, he knows what goes on there. We only know enough to disbelieve what the BBC tells us."

"But my dear fellow, Chatham! Honestly—"

"Sarge, you won't get on in the Force unless you learn to listen and not interrupt with silly remarks. According to Millbank's BBC contacts, there's a tie-up between Warren and Chatham that no one understands, and Miss Mannerton was such a bad secretary that no one would have tolerated her unless they had to. She was blackmailing them, and they manoeuvred her to that window and shot her."

"But look, Chatham got shot too."

"Yes. I'm very grateful to you, sarge, for reminding me except that before you interrupted I was just coming to that. Long ago when you were lying in your silk-lined cradle two men in my platoon shot themselves in the foot with their rifles to get out of those damn awful trenches in Flanders. I'd let my accomplice shoot me in the arm if I had to, to get a blackmailer off my back. No, don't interrupt again, I'll ask the questions and answer them. Who plugged Chatham in the arm? Answer, Warren did. Where from? Chatham's apartment at Imperial Mansions, where else could he take careful aim with a damn great rifle without being seen? And Chatham's slypuss of a wife was there watching him, she's in it too . . .

"Next question: Who shot Miss Mannerton? Chatham did. No, don't interrupt, sarge, you really must learn to listen. Yes, I know Chatham has an alibi, given by his slypuss of a wife. I wasn't quite straight with you when I said I ought to go to Fontbury and check their gunroom as a formality. I went to have a cosy chat with the servants. There are two housemaids, sisters. It happened on their half-day off. There's a butler. He was out that day too, but he snapped my head off when I tried to find out why he and the maids were out of the house at the same time. The cook was in, miles away from the posh part of the house down a long passage. None of them had a good word to say for Mrs Slypuss, but they seemed to think Chatham was okay and the cook thinks he's a very nice gentleman. In the end I got out of her that he had a row with his wife that afternoon. She could hear them shouting at each other from the far end of the house, and then there was a lot of door-slamming when he stomped out and started up his car, and it turned out he'd given her a black eye, which cook thought she richly deserved. Oh dear, did you want to say something?"

"Er, no," said Verney.

"Well done, you're learning to keep your trap shut. Here's the interesting bit. Chatham's car is a silver-grey Delage straight-eight, there can't be more than a dozen of them in the country. Half the village must have seen it drive up the village street and in at a damn great gate at the end with stone birds on and ironwork and all that. But it was getting dark and perhaps the headlights were on and those big sports cars have high doors and only a slit of window at the top. Everyone saw the car, but nobody saw Chatham. Mrs Slypuss says she did, and the cook thought she heard him, but one man yelling his head off at the far end of a long stone passage sounds very like another . . .

"Last question. Why did Mrs Slypuss Chatham let Warren give her a black eye and pretend it was Chatham? It was the least she could do when her husband had let himself be shot at for the good of the cause. He had to have a cast-iron alibi for Miss Mannerton's murder . . .

"I've noted down the mileages, here they are. I reckon Warren would have time in a car like that to drive to Fontbury between Royal Lodge and keeping his appointment in Oxford. He was at Fontbury less than half an hour, from what the cook says. If you want to make yourself useful, sarge, you can persuade Galbraith to get on to the Palace and check 'just as a formality, mind you' what time Warren left Royal Lodge."

"But Galbraith would think I'm mad," Verney bleated.

"Don't tell him why, sarge. We experienced policemen never tell inspectors anything we don't have to."

"You can't prove any of this, old chap, can you?"

"I can try," said Burton.

But it would be a formidable task, Burton realised that. Where, for instance, had Chatham left the Delage for Warren to collect it and drive, first to Royal Lodge, then to Fontbury? In some lock-up garage, perhaps. That would be a convenient place to put on whatever disguise he used in order to avoid being recognised at the Langham Hotel. But there must be hundreds of lock-up garages to let in the western half of London. He would never find the right one. And even if he did he would need a witness who had seen Warren drive the Delage out of it.

George Otway stared in perplexity at the row of lock-up garages behind Number Five Princess of Wales Avenue. In his pocket was a carefully composed letter telling Warren exactly what would happen if he did not get his job back. He had tried once more to telephone Jennifer Howe but the switchboard said girls in the typing pool weren't allowed to take personal calls. The telephone book yielded no Peter Warren living in Battersea. But it occurred to him that even if Warren did not live in the block of flats the garages belonged to, the porter there would know the addresses of people who rented them. Warren probably lived in one of the neighbouring blocks.

But the porter claimed crossly to know nothing about the tenants of the garages. Otway tried one or two other blocks of flats nearby with no result. There was no help for it. He would have to get up early in the morning and mount guard at Broadcasting House so that he could hand the letter to Jennifer Howe when she arrived for work.

At the street end of the carriageway along the side of the block he paused. This was where Warren had nudged him back into the road with the radiator of the Delage. What right had a man like that to a straight-eight Delage? George's hatred of Warren was compounded with envy, the lust of a young man with an engineering background for a superb car. It had a real radiator, not one of those showy chromium shells with a lot of cheap ironmongery hidden behind it. He was sure of that. During the confrontation with Warren he had touched it and it was hot.

Suddenly it occurred to him to wonder. Warren had driven the Delage less than twenty yards from the lock-up garage. Why was its radiator hot?

Harold Millbank was baffled. His undercover sources at Broadcasting House insisted that there was some mysterious secret relationship between Chatham, Warren and Lavinia Mannerton. Chatham and Lavinia Mannerton had both been in Madrid the previous winter consorting with the Spanish Republicans. But Warren had not, how did he fit in? And what about these threatening letters to Chatham that no one was allowed to see? The BBC's pro-Republican and anti-Franco bias was notorious, what was it covering up? Somehow all this must be woven into a publishable story which convicted the BBC of complicity with the Spanish Reds, avoided libel risks, and was credible enough to stand up however fiercely the BBC denied it.

What were the police doing? Officially their lips were sealed, they were part of the great British conspiracy to keep all the skeletons in their cupboards and protect national institutions from disrepute. He had tried to extract information on the side from a disgruntled detective-constable called Burton, but Burton had got more from him than he had given in exchange. His enquiries about Chatham via the country house servants' gossip network had produced only a bit of comic relief. At the moment when Lavinia Mannerton was shot in mistake for Chatham, Chatham had been busy bashing his wife at Fontbury.

Surprisingly the servants' gossip network had produced an interesting sidelight on Warren. He was known to it as a weekend guest in the shooting season, and disliked as a pincher of housemaids' bottoms and worse. Even the gentry seemed to think him rather common. But most of them were hard up and trying desperately to let their shooting, which meant that the game book had to show evidence of massive slaughter in the previous season. Warren was tolerated because he was a first-class shot.

Fontbury was among the houses Warren had stayed in, and he

and Chatham had been contemporaries at Repton. But his visits had ceased at about the time when Millbank's BBC sources reported growing tension between him and Chatham. Warren had to fit in with the Spanish scene somehow. But how?

The telephone interrupted these thoughts. "Yes, that's me . . . Yes, I'd be interested, who's speaking please? Okay if you prefer, but you can trust me to protect my sources and if I don't know who you are the paper can't send you your Christmas present . . . Okay, go ahead. A junior engineer? I'll just take a note of the name. Yes, I do agree, they can't be allowed to get away with this sort of thing. Let's have the details . . ."

The call ended and Millbank looked at the note he had made. Just like the BBC to sack a junior engineer for drunkenness because some prankster had put whisky in his beer. An appeal to the Director-General was pending, but Reith was away, basking in the admiration of some foreign broadcasting organisation or lobbying to land himself an even grander job. Why should the wretched Otway be treated differently from Lieutenant-Commander Woodrooffe, who had got sloshed at the Spithead Review and maundered on about how "the fleet'sh all lit up" till finally the duty announcer and the control room got together and cut him off? Was there one law for the star broadcasters and another for the scullions? It was high time the BBC stopped being so bloody paternalist and its cringing servile staff stopped saying that because everyone had access to Reith and Reith was fair they didn't want a trade union . . . But the words "trade union" would upset the proprietor. When he wrote the piece he must remember to put "proper staff representation" instead.

Before he wrote the piece he must find this man Otway and question him. As he gathered his things and put on his coat it occurred to him that he had heard the voice on the phone before. Whose was it?

Chatham came out of the phone box at his club feeling pleased with himself. His tidbit of anti-BBC dirt had made Millbank salivate with excitement, he could be relied on to go on the rampage in his radio column and get Otway into even worse odour with the top brass at the BBC. Leaks to the press about staff grievances always infuriated them. They assumed automatically that if the aggrieved party had not tipped off the press himself he had undoubtedly put up some crony to do so. When Millbank had finished with Otway Broadcasting House would be as firmly shut to him as the gates of heaven to Lucifer. After a few days of unemployment and despair he would be ready to listen to proposals for keeping his mouth shut from Warren.

The Otway mishap was a nuisance. So was the collapse of the mythical Irishman after so much effort had been lavished on him. Chatham was very annoyed at having suffered a painful wound in the arm to no purpose. But as he had pointed out to Angela and Peter their main defensive position was still intact. All three of them had sound alibis for the time of Lavinia's murder and the police had no reason to suspect a conspiracy between them. To make doubly sure they had evacuated the Marlow cottage after polishing every surface in it that would hold a fingerprint. Barring further accidents they were still safe.

"There's one other item," said the Commodore. "Miss Packard, don't minute this. It's about the Chatham affair."

The senior executives round the table perked up. So far the agenda had been a dreary waste of "nice points" in finance and administration.

"For reasons that I won't go into," the Commodore went on, "and which I don't think are well founded, the police have developed a theory that the attacks on Tony Chatham were a blind and that the intention all the time was to kill Miss Mannerton. They believe that Miss Mannerton was a blackmailer in a substantial way of business and that one of her victims killed her. They suggest that this killer may have been a member of staff."

A ripple of concern went round the table. Everyone surveyed the rich pasture which the BBC with its austere ethic presented to a blackmailer. Irregularities which would pass unnoticed elsewhere could end a promising career, and there was even a couple who had married secretly and defied the Corporation rule that women who got married must resign. They called each other "Miss Smith" and

"Mr Jones" all day and left for their home in the evening at different times. Almost everyone in the room was closing his eyes to, or carefully not knowing about, something of the kind.

"To come to the point," said the Commodore. "The police have asked us to think carefully whether we know of anything to suggest that a member of staff might have been blackmailed, and if so to let them know. I'm sure you all realise that this needs handling very carefully. In an organisation our size there are bound to be one or two black sheep, and some of us may know of, hrrrm, regrettable situations, people who might have exposed themselves to blackmail. But I don't think this is an occasion for spreading out all the Corporation's dirty linen and exhibiting it to the police, with the risk of it finding its way into the press. On the other hand we mustn't appear to be uncooperative, so if anyone has *definite evidence* of any staff member being blackmailed, we ought to pass it on."

There was a long, thoughtful pause. "Andrew Hotchkiss was being blackmailed," said Helen Thackeray. "That was why he killed himself."

"Oh surely not," the Commodore objected. "He had a nervous breakdown, that came out very clearly at the inquest."

"I'm afraid the background was rather more complex," said Helen. "As you know, he was in my department."

"Quite. But I wonder, Helen, if we'd be wise to reopen that very distressing case with the police?"

"We wouldn't be reopening it, they knew perfectly well what had happened but they were very nice about it. If we tell them we can't think of any instances of blackmail they'll decide we're not cooperating. Failing to mention Andrew Hotchkiss would be evidence of bad faith."

Most of those present knew what this was about. Hotchkiss' bank account showed massive withdrawals of cash shortly before he died and the conclusion was obvious. Thanks to some smart BBC fixing nothing but nervous stress had been mentioned at the inquest and Hotchkiss had figured in the press as yet another BBC employee hounded to despair by his half-mad tyrant of a Director-General. This had not bothered Reith at all. He had probably foreseen it and preferred it to the unthinkable alternative of letting suggestions of homosexual sin cloud the BBC's reputation.

That was the sort of reason why Helen Thackeray admired Reith more than any man she knew.

After trudging round Central London for hours for want of something better to do, George Otway was walking up a depressing north London street towards his even more depressing rooming-house. As he climbed the front steps a weaselly-looking man in a camel-hair overcoat and snap-brim hat accosted him.

"Mr Otway?"

"Aye. What's up?"

"I heard about the BBC firing you. Bad business, eh?"

"Aye . . ." said George, and waited.

"Care to tell me about it? I might be able to help."

"Who are you then?"

The stranger produced a visiting card. George took one look at it and handed it back. "I'm not talking to the press," he said and tried to dodge past into the house.

"Hey, wait," cried Harold Millbank.

But George knew he must not talk to reporters for fear of prejudicing his appeal to the DG. He brushed Millbank off and ran into the house, slamming the door behind him.

This upsetting incident made him forget to wonder why the radiator of Warren's Delage had been so hot.

An enterprising publisher had sent Helen Thackeray an advance copy of yet another book about the Spanish Civil War, a rather good eyewitness account by a boy of seventeen of one of the early battles, in which he had fought on the Republican side. The suggestion was that it would make good broadcast material, but that was out of the question. She had done her best to give the war even-handed coverage and any more publicity for the Republican cause would provoke yet another anguished protest from Vansittart at the Foreign Office, to the effect that the BBC's implacable hostility to Franco was driving him into the arms of Hitler and Mussolini.

Though there was no question of using the book Helen went on reading it out of personal interest. The writer, young Esmond Romilly, had been in a small group of British volunteers attached to the Thaelmann Battalion of anti-Nazi Germans. Romilly gave character sketches of many of his British companions in arms but not, to her surprise, of the one she was interested in, Tony Chatham's nephew Michael. No doubt he thought it kinder to the Chatham family and to the Republican cause to keep quiet about a man who had been shot as a spy, probably as the result of a ludicrous mistake. That must have happened towards the end of November. In December what was left of the Romilly group of Britons got involved, with the remains of the Thaelmann Battalion, in another bloody battle north-west of Madrid at a village called Boadilla. And amid the tumult of house-to-house fighting the Romilly group had a surprise encounter with another small body of British volunteers headed by John Cornford. They were machine gunners attached to the André Marty Battalion, which had been fighting on a different front. Romilly had heard vague reports of their existence, but *this was the first time that the two groups had met.*

Helen Thackeray read the paragraph again carefully. She was one of the few women who had climbed out of the throng of middle-rank female staff into the area at the top of the BBC which was a closely but unobtrusively guarded male preserve. This was partly due to an alert curiosity, and it was aroused now. How had John Cornford come to know that Michael Chatham, far from being a dead hero, had been shot as a fascist spy? Had Esmond Romilly had time to tell him during that brief encounter, interrupted by bursts of gunfire from the shattered village? Yet Chatham said he had heard the story of his nephew's fate from John Cornford. Perhaps it was a slip of the tongue.

THIRTEEN

"Good morning, Miss," said George Otway, blocking the pavement in front of Jennifer.

She had almost forgotten about the ox-like young man with the ill-fitting suit and plastered hair who wanted a letter delivered to Peter Warren. She took it from him quickly. It was almost nine, she would be late for work.

"You won't just leave it on his desk, Miss, will you? It's private."

"No, I'll hand it to him myself," she promised, and turned to go.

"One moment, Miss. You wouldn't . . . come to a cinema with me this evening?"

Foreseeing complications and embarrassment Jennifer opened her mouth to decline.

"Or tomorrow night if you're busy," he added.

Unless she was brutal, she would have to invent a different excuse for every night of the week. Either way he would be hurt and think her snobbish. In the BBC's social pecking order even junior secretaries ranked well above programme engineers.

"Please Miss. I can't stay in my digs all day, and it's lonely wandering round London with nothing to do. I lost my job at the BBC."

"Oh, I suppose that's what you're writing to Mr Warren about?"

"That's right," said George cautiously. "I reckon he may help."

That made the whole thing more understandable, and a brush-off more difficult. "Very well, let's go to a cinema tonight. But you must let me pay for myself, I insist."

"Oh no, Miss," said George, inexpressibly shocked. "I couldn't allow that."

"Well, we'll see," said Jennifer, resigning herself to a sticky evening. She found out his name, agreed on a time and place to meet, and hurried into Broadcasting House.

George stared after her in open admiration. With nothing to do all day he had thought a great deal about her. It would never come to anything, of course. She was a lady and he was not a gentleman. But she had agreed to come out with him, that was a feather in his cap. He felt almost cheerful.

Back at Oxford Circus he bought a newspaper and went into a teashop. A cup of tea and a newspaper would kill two hours. After that he would go to the Labour Exchange.

He always began reading the paper at the football and worked backwards towards the front page. Somewhere about the middle his eye was caught by the words "BBC sacking" and "too terrorised to speak out". He read on. There, sickeningly, was his own name. This was about him.

Millbank had been fair, to the extent of making it clear that this latest victim of the BBC's "Prussian" attitude to its staff had refused to speak to him, having been "terrorised" by the usual threats of dire penalties if he aired his grievance in the press. But that hardly mattered. The whole tone of the article was deeply offensive to the BBC management. Reith would turn his appeal down flat. Who had given Millbank his information? It was obvious. Warren had pulled yet another dirty trick.

George Otway was still muttering curses against Warren into his teacup when Jennifer Howe slipped out of the typing pool with his letter and knocked on Warren's door. One of Warren's shirt buttons was undone, she could see his bulging vest. He looked rather ill. A girl she had never seen before was sitting at Lavinia's desk.

When she handed Warren the letter he tore it open and read rapidly. With a glance at Lavinia's successor he drew Jennifer out into the passage.

"Where did you get this?" he muttered.

"He gave it to me and asked me to hand it to you personally."

"D'you know him then?"

"Yes."

"How well?"

This was enough to make her boil over. "Mr Warren, I can't imagine what business that can possibly be of yours," she snapped, and turned on her heel. She was furious. She knew the work of the Features Unit and had held the fort competently in Chatham's office during a time of great stress. Yet when it came to replacing Lavinia they had left her sweating away like a galley-slave in the typing pool and got in a strange girl from nowhere. She was still being punished, she realised, for having stuck to her guns and insisted on telling the police about Lavinia's fatal phone call.

She had been too angry to notice, but as they spoke Warren's cheeks had gone grey and he had put his hand to his lips to stop them trembling. The moment she had gone he lurched along the passage to Chatham's office. His battleaxe of a temporary secretary was there too but that could not be allowed to matter. The disaster was too urgent. He handed the letter to Chatham in silence.

Chatham read it. "Peter, this is a dreadful muddle, isn't it? I do wish you'd be more careful."

Automatically he had used the tone of sorrowful, friendly rebuke which he kept for junior producers who had done something rather silly. It infuriated Warren who launched out into a panic-stricken tirade. It was no more his fault than Chatham's, he had merely followed the policy which Chatham had laid down . . .

"Violet, would you be very kind and get us some coffee?" Chatham interrupted. "Mr Warren likes two lumps and very little milk."

It was in character for him and Warren to quarrel in front of third parties. But Warren was in a bad way. At any moment he might say too much.

As the hennaed battleaxe rose and departed he handed George Otway's letter back to Warren. "Now, Peter, what's the trouble? We expected something like this and decided how to handle it."

"The point is, this semi-literate piece of nastiness was handed to me by Jennifer Howe. *She knows him.*"

Chatham's face froze. "How well?"

"I asked her," said Warren in a terrified mutter. "She snarled at me and said it was none of my business and stalked off."

"Had you said or done anything to annoy her?"

"No, I swear I hadn't. No hand on the knee, nothing. Otway must have told her the whole story about his sister and put her against me. What the hell do we do, we're right in the cart now."

Before Chatham could answer the door opened and Helen Thackeray walked in. She had not knocked. There was no reason why anyone of her seniority should.

She glanced from Chatham to Warren. "I'm sorry, am I interrupting something?"

Chatham threw her his usual welcoming smile. "No. Just business as usual."

"I was wondering if you'd used Harold Nicolson lately. I hear rumours of drink."

"There are rumours," said Chatham, "but not about drink."

"Oh. Then it must have been beautiful young men and I misunderstood. I wish people would say what they mean."

She prepared to linger. Chatham and Warren waited tensely for her to go.

"You two seem to have a problem. Can I help at all?"

"Bless you, but I think we can handle it," said Chatham.

The door closed behind her.

"Damn it, how much did she hear?" whispered Warren.

"Nothing. Top BBC ladies don't listen at keyholes."

"Damn everything. What do we do about Jennifer Howe and Otway?"

Chatham thought. "Go down to the typing pool and say we want to contact Otway urgently. Say it's about fixing him up with a job and ask if she knows where we can contact him today."

"And then what?"

"I have to rehearse the feature for tonight, but I shall break for lunch as early as I can. You can tell me then what you've found out."

"You mean, you'll be in the studio all day? You can't!"

"I must, we've got to keep up a front of business as usual. Do pull yourself together."

"Are you sure Ma Thackeray didn't hear anything?"

"Yes. Hurry."

Chatham had a few minutes before he needed to go to the studio and meet the cast, and began running his eye over the script he would be producing: *Turning Points. An anthology of prose and verse inspired by life's moments of decision.* One of Browning's *Dramatic Lyrics*, Kutuzov in *War and Peace* deciding to abandon Moscow, scraps of Shakespeare and Christina Rossetti, T. S. Eliot's *Journey of the Magi*, Trollope's henpecked Bishop of Barchester revolting at last against his monstrous wife . . . rather a ragbag really. He had thrown the thing together in a hurry to fill an unexpected gap in the schedule. Fortunately it would be plain sailing to produce.

Violet was talking to someone on the telephone. "I'm sorry, no. She doesn't work here now, she's been transferred to another office. Who's speaking, please? . . . Very well, Inspector Galbraith. I'll have you transferred to the typing pool Supervisor, she'll be able to arrange an appointment for you to see Miss Howe."

Chatham had stopped looking through the script, which had become a blur on the desk in front of him. How well did Jennifer know George Otway? Had Otway told her about his dealings with Warren? If so, she would certainly think the story worth repeating to the police.

He pulled himself together. Business as usual. He must concentrate and not make a fool of himself on the air as Warren had done over Vasco da Gama. He took a deep breath and strode into the studio.

"Good morning, everyone, shall we start with a run through just to get the feel of it? Anthea, would you and Geoffrey take this mike, and the others can work to the far one . . ." Professional discipline took over, forcing him to listen to the balance of voices and keep the pace lively and full of contrasts. The Christina Rossetti would have to come out, the mood was wrong. He would substitute a music bridge. They were treating Darcy's proposal to Elizabeth Bennet as high tragedy, making far too heavy weather of it. He pressed the talk-back key.

"Anthea and Geoffrey, could you make it a bit lighter and more informal? *Pride and Prejudice* is a comedy, after all. If you'd just take that line again, Anthea?"

"Mr Darcy," Anthea repeated in a drawing-room comedy tone,

"you could not have made me the offer of your hand in any possible way that would have tempted me to accept it."

Why, Chatham wondered, had Jennifer Howe suddenly decided to hate Peter Warren? Otway must have poisoned her mind against him, told her the whole unpleasant story, from the dumping on Wimbledon Common to the beer laced with whisky. This was worrying. So far Otway had been relatively harmless because he did not know that Lavinia had been concerned in his sister's abortion. He had no reason to suppose that the police would be interested in his grievance against Warren, as suggesting a possible murder motive. But if Jennifer passed on what Otway had told her to the police, they would realise at once that Otway was a person they ought to question. Then the fat would be in the fire . . . He jerked back to attention as a new voice began intoning through the far mike:

> "There is a tide in the affairs of men,
> Which, taken at the flood, leads on to fortune;
> Omitted, all the voyage of their life
> Is bound in shallows and in miseries . . ."

Hell, why did I put in that hackneyed bit of Bard, he thought. He had taken the tide at the flood and unless a miracle happened he would be on the rocks.

The Otway angle was only one of the dangers and not the worst. He cursed himself for being too thorough. He had taken Jennifer Howe down into the underground garage at Dolphin Square to impress on her mind the image of him driving off in the Delage to deal with the crisis at Fontbury. Twenty minutes later George Otway had seen Warren drive an identical car out of a lock-up garage less than a mile from Dolphin Square. If the conversation between Jennifer and Otway turned to sports cars (it might, he was probably that sort of young man) then Chatham's alibi for Lavinia's murder would be blown sky-high. For the first time he was really afraid.

*

Halfway through typing the programme-as-broadcast for the previous afternoon, a waste of cinema organs and cookery talks, Jennifer glanced up and saw Warren's ashen face staring at her across her typewriter. He was still clutching George Otway's letter.

"You know what's in this?" he asked hoarsely.

"He's lost his job and hopes you'll help," said Jennifer coldly. "I assume it's about that."

Was she lying? What else had Otway told her? Somehow Warren managed to keep up a front. "That's absolutely right, yes, and I've just happened to hear of a job that might suit him, but he'll have to apply double-quick. D'you know where I can get hold of him?"

"He's meeting me at half past six here at reception to go to a cinema."

"And earlier?"

"I think he wanders about most of the day, rather than sit in his digs. You could have a word with him at half past six when he meets me, if that would do."

It would not do. At all costs Jennifer and Otway must be kept apart. "The trouble is, it would take me some time, explaining what the job is and feeding him the right things to say at the interview. Could I be an unmitigated spoilsport and suggest that I meet him instead of you? It's important for him, I'd like to take him away and brief him properly. I could say I'd seen you and you'd agreed to go out with him some other time instead."

"Very well, arrange it as you think best," said Jennifer, none too graciously. "Make it tomorrow night if he's free."

Warren hurried away. He and Chatham would have to put their heads together and plan something pretty drastic. But first he needed a stiff drink. Twelve-thirty. There was time for a quick dive into the Stag's Head while Chatham was still rehearsing.

When he got back Chatham was sitting behind his desk in a cold fury waiting for him.

"Where have you been?"

"I'm sorry." There was nothing Warren dreaded more than Chatham's icy anger.

"You've been drinking," Chatham snapped. "Stop it and pull yourself together, you've done quite enough harm already. What did you get out of Jennifer?"

Warren told him.

"Right. Send your girl to lunch early, I can't keep shooing Violet out of the room and I want to phone."

Warren obeyed. "Phone who?"

"Anyone who will give Otway an interview, to convince him that you're trying to help him. Let's try the Australians first."

He put a call through to the London representative of the Australian Broadcasting Commission.

"Dick? Has ABC any vacancies for programme engineers?"

"No idea. Want me to find out?"

"Not yet, but would you do me a favour and interview a lad who's down on his luck? Just to give his morale a boost, he's had a raw deal here, but you needn't commit yourself . . . Thanks a lot, I'll give you the background . . ."

He explained about the lacing of Otway's beer as a "practical joke" which went wrong. Warren fidgeted till the call ended.

"Tony, getting him interviews won't keep him away from Jennifer. We need to be far more drastic."

"How d'you mean, drastic?"

"Well—"

"If you mean what I think you mean, you're crazy. If he's talked to Jennifer already and Jennifer's passed it all on to the police, they'll know who to blame for anything that happens to Otway. D'you want to hang for two murders instead of one?"

Warren turned a delicate shade of green.

"All we can do is hope they haven't talked much yet," Chatham went on, "and keep them apart. Let's think. The electric wiring at your love nest cottage looked pretty ropey to me, we might build something on that. Hey—where are you going?"

"To throw up," said Warren.

Among Helen Thackeray's qualifications for high office was an integrity which did not allow her friendships with colleagues to cloud her judgment. When she walked in unexpectedly that morning on Chatham and Warren she had overheard nothing. But she had seen the guilty look of conspiracy on their faces and realised for the first time that Chatham's warm friendly smile was a performance that could be switched on.

Once a train of thought had started it had to be followed through, however unwelcome the direction it might lead in. She made herself face the fact that the relationship between Chatham and Warren had always mystified her a little. She had never quite understood why Chatham had fought so hard to have a flashy, argumentative producer from another department as his deputy in preference to two strong candidates in his own. She had let him have his way when he insisted that they were both "too pedestrian". But was that the real reason?

There was an even more disquieting angle to the same mystery. Warren's predecessor in the deputy post had left behind him a competent and agreeable secretary. Chatham, not Warren, had mounted an unobtrusive and highly sophisticated intrigue to get her moved, in order to create a vacancy for a substitute who was neither competent nor agreeable: Lavinia Mannerton, of all people.

Helen owed some of this knowledge to her own secretary, who kept a discreet ear to the ground on her behalf but never repeated mere gossip. From the same source she had learnt that some mystery surrounded a young woman called Jennifer Howe, who had acted as a relief in Chatham's office just before Lavinia Mannerton was murdered. Helen remembered her as quiet and intelligent. But despite the two vacancies in Warren's and Chatham's offices she had not been considered for either post, nor indeed for any post outside the typing pool. Why not?

Like every BBC employee including Helen herself, Jennifer Howe had a personal file which contained everything the Corporation had on record about her, but which she herself would never see. As was her right, Helen sent for it. The last entry was a report by Tony Chatham on her performance as his relief secretary: "Satisfactory on the whole. But she tends to mishear or misunderstand instructions and make muddles." But before the murder Chatham had said more than once that he thought highly of her.

The remarks put on the file by Amy Proctor of Features Executive were far more scathing than Chatham's. There certainly was a mystery here. On the principle that one got more out of people face to face than on the telephone, Helen marched into Amy Proctor's office, affecting not to notice the cosmetics being swept hastily into a desk drawer. What went on, she wondered in passing, in the mind of a middle-aged woman who spent hours every day waging war on her own appearance?

"Hullo, Amy. Tell me, what happened to that nice quiet girl who was in Tony Chatham's office for a bit, Jennifer something? There's a vacancy coming up next month in Topical Talks and she might do nicely."

"Oh no. I'm sorry, Miss Thackeray, I couldn't recommend her."

"Really? What's wrong with her?"

"She tried to make herself seem important after the murder by inventing a ridiculous story and telling it to the police."

"Dear me, what about?"

"Oh, something about overhearing a phone call just before Lavinia Mannerton was shot."

Helen mastered the details, and decided that the "ridiculous story" was not ridiculous at all. It fitted in uncomfortably well among the awkward ideas which were surging up from her unconscious. And there was something else she meant to ask Amy Proctor, something she would rather not know, since it would probably shatter her peace of mind. But she had a scholar's conscience, and it would not keep quiet.

"Oh, there's one other thing, Amy. I'm trying to fix the date of something that Tony Chatham and I tried to fix up last winter in the 'Great Explorers' series. I think it was just after he got back from that leave he took, but I don't want to bother him. Could you just look up his leave dates last December?"

As she had feared, the answer destroyed what remained of her mental calm. "Thank you, Amy," she murmured, and went back to her office to think.

According to Romilly's book, he had heard rumours that another group of British volunteers was involved in the fighting round Madrid during November 1936. But he had not met them until the second day of the Boadilla battle, when he was recognised and hailed by one of them, the communist poet John Cornford.

When Helen first read the book this passage had left her faintly uneasy. According to Tony Chatham his nephew had been shot as a spy, a fact he had learnt from this same John Cornford. How did Cornford know, she had asked herself. One had to imagine that Romilly had found time to tell him in the intervals of murderous house-to-house fighting for possession of a shattered village. But now the improbable had become the impossible. She had checked with the back files of the newspapers. The Boadilla battle started on 13th December. Tony Chatham left Madrid on the 14th, the day on which Cornford met Romilly. He could not have repeated anything Romilly told him to Chatham.

Moreover Cornford had been killed a fortnight after the Boadilla battle. Chatham had given as his authority a source which could not be checked. Disjointed facts began forming an alarming pattern in Helen's mind.

FOURTEEN

JENNIFER STOOD WAITING in Chatham's office, trying not to look
at the spot where she had found Lavinia lying dead. A message had
come down to the typing pool that Chatham wanted to see her at
the end of his afternoon rehearsal. Curiosity was her main reaction.

"Ah hullo, Jennifer," he said, hurrying in. The warm smile
implied that she was the one person he had been longing to see all
day, but she was in no mood to take it at its face value. As long as
she was doing penance in the typing pool, everyone in Features
Unit and Features Executive was double faced.

"Oh, before I forget," he began. "The police rang here this
morning asking to talk to you. Did they make contact all right?"

"Yes. Inspector Galbraith came to ask me some more questions
just before lunch."

"Oh really?" said Chatham, tensely offhand. "Do they seem to
be making any headway?"

So that's it, thought Jennifer. The management had detailed
him to question her discreetly and find out if she was still persisting
in her "ridiculous story" about the phone call.

"I don't think so," she replied. "They asked me the same old
questions more or less, and I gave them the same old answers."
There was no need to tell him that she had also been asked,
puzzlingly, to give as detailed a description as she could of
Chatham's car.

Greatly relieved, Chatham passed on to his next business.
"What I really wanted to say was, you've been on my conscience.
You did a marvellous job for me during that awful time, I was so
grateful. You're much too good to be wasted in that deadly typing
pool."

"Thank you," said Jennifer, but remained on her guard.

"The hellish thing is, though, I have to go back to the studio and give out my notes to the cast. Look, are you free for dinner tomorrow night? We could go somewhere quiet and have a talk."

Good gracious me, she thought, a wolf in sheep's clothing. She was damned if she'd sit in a restaurant with a married man who'd quarrelled with his wife and let him put his hand up her skirt. If he wanted to get her out of the pool, why had he not arranged for her to be given Lavinia's job?

"I'm sorry, I have a date tomorrow," she said, not knowing or caring whether this was true.

Exactly, with Otway, Chatham told himself. It sounded as if Otway had told her very little so far, all might yet be well if they could be kept apart.

He produced a sad, pleading smile. "Oh dear, can't you cancel it? Tomorrow's the only night I have free this week."

He waited for her to say "yes". To judge from the agitated concern for his safety she had shown in the Dolphin Square garage, she was in love with him, his secretaries usually were, and on top of that she was dead keen to get out of the typing pool. Over dinner he would make some mild sexual advance to keep her interested and poison her mind against Otway, so that she steered clear of him for good.

But being hopelessly miscast as a bold seducer he had overdone the winsome smile. Jennifer watched it degenerate into a fixed grimace which suggested that heavy breathing would begin at any moment.

"Do put the other chap off," he pleaded.

"I'm sorry, it's a date that's been postponed once already," she said, finding to her surprise that this happened to be true.

"What a pity. I did so want to help," said Chatham.

"In that case," she snapped, "we'd better discuss it in the office some time. Good night, Mr Chatham."

She turned on her heel and marched out. The arrogance, she thought, how dare he look astonished and angry when she turned him down? Like the Caliph of Baghdad glaring at a third-rate dancing girl who had just said "no". It would have served him right if she had stung him for an expensive dinner and slapped his face when the funny business began. She would have too, but for her postponed date with Otway.

Chatham was disagreeably surprised, but also puzzled. He had made no explicitly immoral proposal, nothing to justify cries of outraged virtue at this stage. What could she possibly have against him? Unless she and Otway had already put their heads together about the Delage and worked out that his alibi was false, but surely that was unthinkable. He would work it out later. What mattered for the moment was how well Peter Warren handled his interview with Otway. Chatham felt he had done a good job on Warren, stiffening his shattered morale and telling him in great detail what line to take. When they parted at the end of the lunch hour Warren had been calm and even quietly confident of his ability to handle the Otway problem. But having to look after a production at the critical moment was a nuisance, because it meant leaving Warren to his own devices in the dangerous hour between opening time at the pubs and his meeting with Otway. Despite Chatham's stern lecture about drink, he was quite capable of stoking up with Dutch courage in the Stag's Head beforehand. If he did, anything might happen.

In the hall at Broadcasting House Warren explained to George Otway that Jennifer was willing to postpone their cinema date "so that we can talk about this letter of yours, though I honestly don't understand it."

"If that's your line there's no use us talking," said George stolidly. "I'll have to tell the DG all about you and Annie when I see him about my appeal."

"Oh no, look, we can come to some arrangement but really, we can't discuss it here, the car's outside."

"The car" was the Delage, lent by Chatham to reinforce George's belief that it was Warren's car. It was parked round the corner in Langham Street. Rain was falling steadily. George climbed in beside Warren. Even with so much on his mind he could not help noticing the glorious luxury of its engineering. All sorts of things like the gear lever were machine-turned when a casting would have done just as well. Beside him, Warren smelt of sweat and drink. His speech just avoided being slurred.

"Where are you taking me then?" George asked as Warren headed north up Portland Place.

"I thought we'd sit in the car, that would do. Somewhere in Regent's Park."

"Suits me," said George. At this time on a rainy night there would be no one about to interfere if he got no satisfaction and decided to give Warren another bashing.

Warren drove on in silence, trying to remember the points Chatham had told him to make. Halfway round the Outer Circle he pulled in to the kerb.

"Now look, I'll tell you first what I won't do. I will not go to Reith and say 'Give Otway his job back, because it was all my fault, I tampered with his drink'."

"You damn well will," George shouted.

"No, because he'd say 'Why on earth did you do that?' and I'd have no answer that didn't land me in the manure-heap. I might as well let you go ahead and make your stink, and then tell Reith you're a liar, you've got no proof, have you?"

"You've got to get me my job back," George insisted. "You've got to speak for me."

"But look, if I go to Reith and say 'Please don't sack Otway' he'll say 'What business is it of yours, he's not in your department. It's between me and Controller Engineering'."

"So you'll do nothing for me," George burst out.

"Yes. I'll get you another job, just as good."

"What sort of job?"

"Listen, a BBC-trained programme engineer can walk into a good job in any broadcasting organisation in the Empire. To start with, I've fixed up an interview for you on Thursday with the London representative of ABC."

"That's no good to me."

"Why not? You'd get promotion in Australia far quicker than you would here. Ten-thirty at their office, ask for Dick Larsen."

"That's no damn good, they'd take up my references and the BBC would say I'd been sacked for coming on duty drunk."

"I càn get round that, I'll explain that it was all a mistake. It may take time, though, and I've a temporary job for you so you don't have to stay on the dole."

"What's that then?"

"Replacing the wiring in my weekend cottage. It's all in old-fashioned wooden conduit, horribly dangerous. I'll give you four pounds a week and you can live there while you're working on it."

"Where is this cottage?"

"In Buckinghamshire. Near Marlow."

No, George thought. He had to be in London, to date Jennifer and job-hunt. This talk of the Empire was rubbish. "I'll take the four pound without the job," he said.

"No, no, that won't do," said Warren. He was desperate. Somehow he had to get Otway to the cottage and keep him there, away from Jennifer. "Tell you what," he added, trying to sound casual, "I'll drive you there now, and you can look at the job and then decide."

He had started the engine and was reaching for the gear lever, but George was not having that. All was clear to him now, he was about to be driven to a remote country cottage and, to use a newish Americanism, bumped off. As Warren's hand reached the gear lever George brought his clenched fist down on it with a thump that drove the knob hard into Warren's palm.

The car was in gear, and Warren, maddened by the pain in his hand, was doing all the wrong things with his feet. The Delage shot forward at full throttle, bounced on and off the kerb, and veered towards the wrong side of the road. Warren seemed to be trying to get it under control, but its magnificent acceleration was too much for him and he managed only to send it into a terrifying skid. At the start of the second complete revolution George gripped the wheel and tried to steer into the skid, but Warren was fighting him all the time. As a last resort he switched off the ignition. The Delage hit the kerb with a sickening thud, lurched heavily but by a miracle did not overturn. George jumped out, ran round it and opened the driver's door, intending to drag Warren out.

"You drunken fornicating bastard," he shouted. "You're getting a lesson from me that you'll never forget."

"That's . . . what you think," said Warren, looking at him with a stunned expression. "Just keep quite still."

George obeyed. It would be silly to argue with the wrong end of a pistol in the hand of a man who was half-sodden with drink.

"Right, everyone," said Chatham, looking round at his cast. "Just a few final points. Anthea, top of page seven, do watch the cue light. You came in early, you were under the music. Andrew, page nine, could you take the Eliot on the near mike, there was a bit of a crowd round that one, engineers make a note of that. And I still think you're being too heavy with the *War and Peace* bit, it's not poetry, it's not even sprung prose, do be a bit more colloquial. We're still twenty seconds over, I want to make another small cut. Would everyone look at page fifteen, please."

Over in the corner of the studio a phone was flashing its light. One of the junior engineers went to answer it, then came back and hovered over Chatham.

"If it's for me I can't talk to anyone," he said and went on explaining about the cut.

But the engineer went on hovering. "It's Mrs Chatham. She says would you phone her please, as soon as you're off the air."

Chatham registered the message, then shut it out of his mind. The minutes were ticking by, soon control room would cue him and *Turning Points* would be on the air. He was damned if he would lose concentration and make a fool of himself in front of the listeners like Warren.

But as the cue came up, there was only one thought in his mind. What on earth had happened at Fontbury? They had agreed not to phone each other except in emergency.

Angela's afternoon had started badly, with a difficult phone call from her brother.

"Angie, old girl, you mustn't weaken," he bellowed. "My blood boils to think of you at the mercy of that brute."

"I suddenly thought, it's a bit drastic. If I divorce him he'll have to resign from the BBC."

"Serve the swine right, you're being far too soft with him."

"We could have that other thing, not living together but not being divorced."

"But Angie, we went into all that. A judicial separation isn't the same thing at all. Supposing you wanted to marry some decent clean-living chap?"

"I could divorce Tony then."

"No no, strike while the iron's hot. You need to cut loose from that unhealthy BBC atmosphere, old girl, poisoning the nation with a lot of left-wing claptrap, you see what the press is saying about him and Red Spain? Tell you what, I've got all the papers here ready for you to sign. I'll bring them over now and if we file the suit now it'll come up early in the spring."

"No, Gerald. Not this afternoon. I'm busy, I have a visitor."

"Get rid of him."

"I don't think that would be possible."

"Why not?"

"It's someone with a problem that needs handling carefully."

"Let me come over and help."

"*No*, Gerald. You're being very stupid and tiresome, you really must learn to take a hint."

"Angie, you're making me damn suspicious. What's going on, is this a bit of hanky-panky with some chap?"

"I don't think you could quite call it hanky-panky, Gerald."

"Then what do you call it? My God, is this why you're funking your fences over the divorce?"

"Well . . ." He could not be told the true reason, and among the available lies his own theory could hardly be improved on. "Hanky-panky is such an ugly word for something rather special."

"Special? What d'you mean, special? Does your husband know?"

"I'm not sure."

After a stunned silence Gerald began roaring down the telephone that she was not to blame him if Chatham divorced her ignominiously, that he would drive over at once to Fontbury to "thrash things out", that he washed his hands of the whole sordid business.

"Then you can wash your hands at home," said Angela. "I'm not having you thrashing about here."

Having disposed of him she crossed the hall to the drawing-room where a tall, grim-faced man in a dark suit rose to greet her.

"Inspector Galbraith? I'm sorry to keep you waiting. My brother was on the phone about the arrangements for my divorce. Do sit down, what can I do for you?"

"I have some questions tae put tae ye, Madam, concerning events at the time of Miss Mannerton's death."

"Oh? I doubt if I can help you, Inspector, but do please go on."

"I need tae check the movements of the parties concerned on the previous day."

"Then I certainly can't help you. My husband wasn't here and of course he doesn't tell me his day-to-day movements anymore."

"I was enquiring intae your movements, Madam."

Angela sat very still. Suddenly Galbraith reminded her of Sir John Reith. "Mine? Oh dear, I'll try to remember. Which day of the week are we talking about?"

"A Thursday, Madam. The fatality occurred on a Friday."

"Oh dear, how difficult. I don't keep a diary."

"Would ye maybe have visited London on that day?"

He knew. It was better to admit it. But how much did he know?

"How clever of you, Inspector. Now I come to think of it, I was in London."

"And what would be the purpose of your journey?"

A safe answer came to her in a flash. "I went to see that big exhibition at Burlington House."

"With a friend, maybe?"

"Oh no, I hate going to exhibitions with someone who keeps saying 'oh do look at this' or 'one sees the influence of Velasquez here'. I always go by myself."

"Did ye not encounter some acquaintance who could confirm that ye were there?"

"Let me see . . . only an awful woman whose name I couldn't remember, she talked about her illnesses."

After one desultory question about the mythical hypochondriac Galbraith waved her aside. "Now, if I was tae suggest that on the day in question a person answering tae your description was seen tae purchase a second-hand Willesden canvas cabin trunk with leather corners, how would ye reply?"

It was all right, he was guessing. When she bought the cabin trunk she was already in the disguise she used at the Langham Hotel, and did not correspond to her own description at all.

"How ridiculous, Inspector, of course not. I must say, you're asking some very odd questions. I think I'm entitled to know what you're driving at."

"Murder is a serious matter. I have tae examine all the possibilities. An innocent person who tells no lies has naething tae fear from me."

Again, he reminded her of Reith. "I'm not afraid, just bewildered. Do please go on."

"Ye say ye did not purchase the trunk that was used tae smuggle the murder weapon intae the Langham Hotel. Did ye visit there?"

"Well, I lunched in September with an aunt who was staying there."

"Ye deliberately misunderstand me, woman. We're speaking of the day before Miss Lavinia Mannerton was murdered."

"I was not at the Langham Hotel on that day. And please stop calling me 'woman', it's rude."

"If ye did not spend the night of Thursday tae Friday in room 457 at the Langham Hotel under the name of Mrs Henry Johnson, where did ye spend it?"

Angela swallowed down panic. If she said "Imperial Mansions" Galbraith would wonder what she was doing in a one-bedroom flat with a man she was purporting to divorce, and when he checked the hall porter would say he had not seen her.

"Your servants tell me," Galbraith went on, "that ye left here with a suitcase on the Thursday morning, and did not return until the forenoon of the following day."

Blessedly, there was a safe answer after all. "Quite right, I borrowed my brother's London flat. He lets me have a key. I'll give you the address."

Galbraith grunted, probably in disbelief, and began taking her through the events of the Friday afternoon: the shouting match, the black eye, the stormy departure for London in the Delage. "It's regrettable," he commented, "that no one but yourself saw Mr Chatham, tae confirm your story."

"I don't understand you at all, Inspector."

"The two maidservants, now. They have Friday, the both of them, as their half day."

"Yes. They're sisters. It's only fair for them to have their time off together."

"But they tell me it was Thursday, till ye changed it a week before the fatality."

"Yes. Let me see, there was a reason. Something to do with their mother and the Women's Institute, I forget the details."

"It appears that on the same Friday ye had a disagreement with your butler, Mr Harrison, shortly after ye returned from. . . . where did ye say? Oh aye, your brother's London flat."

"Yes. Harrison was very impertinent."

"And ye ordered him tae leave the house."

"Oh dear, one says these things when one's angry. I didn't think he'd take it literally."

"But he did. Was it not convenient tae ye, and part of a deliberate plan, that everyone but the cook in her faraway kitchen should be elsewhere at the time ye say Mr Chatham called here?"

There was a very long pause.

"I could help you more," said Angela with a wicked edge to her voice, "if I knew what you're trying to prove. If you won't tell me, I shall have to get my brother, who is the Lord Lieutenant of Wiltshire, to find out."

"There'll be no need for that, Mrs Chatham, I'll be open with ye. I'm attempting to establish that your husband has an alibi for Miss Mannerton's murder, and I canna say that I'm succeeding."

FIFTEEN

"ANGIE? YOU LEFT a message asking me to phone," said Chatham.

"Oh. Yes," said Angela coldly. They had to be careful. The hand-operated exchange in the village was manned by Mrs Harper, the postmistress, who listened in to calls likely to prove interesting and did not always keep her harvest of gossip to herself. Further news of the Chatham divorce was high on her list of priorities, and they had evolved a rough and ready code, rather like a bidding convention at bridge, to frustrate her.

"Could you be at the lawyers at eleven?" Angela asked. "There's something we both have to sign, and it's rather urgent."

She had not said "eleven tomorrow". Under the convention, that meant eleven tonight. What on earth had happened?

"I think I could manage that," he said, and waited for the next round of bidding, which would tell him where.

"And there's a card here saying that they've finished repairing your watch. Can you call in and collect it?"

"Let me see, which watchmaker did we take it to?"

"The one opposite Hammersmith tube station."

"Very well, I'll see to that. Anything else?"

"No."

For the benefit of Mrs Harper, agog at her switchboard, they bade each other a cold goodnight. He looked at his watch. It was well after nine. She would have to drive hell for leather if she was to meet him at Hammersmith tube station at eleven. Whatever had happened must have upset her a lot.

As was proper for a former headmaster of Repton, Helen Thackeray's brother Robert had recently become a Bishop. By dint of some brisk telephoning she tracked him down to the Athenaeum and had him summoned from the smoking room to talk to her.

"Of course I remember them," he said in answer to her query. "They were inseparable, right from their first term. Warren was the showoff, everyone thought of him as the dominant partner. Chatham was the quiet clever one, I think he enjoyed manipulating Warren without Warren realising . . ."

The character sketch went on for some time before Helen could put the question that really interested her.

"Were they both in the OTC, Robert?"

"Of course." He sounded surprised. Public schoolboys were by definition good officer material. Only conscientious objectors failed to join the school's Officer Training Corps, and they were given rather a bad time.

"So I suppose they were taught to shoot?" she persisted.

"My dear Helen, they were both crack shots. Repton won the Ashburton Shield at Bisley for three years' running while they were in the team."

Helen thanked the Bishop and added this item to the stock of information she would have preferred not to know. If Chatham had competed at Bisley he must know enough to have realised at once that the shot which wounded him in the arm came from a rifle, not a shotgun. Did he really believe that his wife had provided herself with a rifle and smuggled it into the flat in order to shoot at him in a moment of anger after a quarrel? If not, why had he pretended to her that he did?

"Sorry, caller, there's no reply," said the operator after a long wait. Chatham left the call box, wondering what on earth had happened. It was the second time he had rung the Marlow cottage. By rights Warren and Otway should have arrived there hours ago.

The call box was outside Barnes Station, in the middle of the common. Jennifer Howe lived in one of the streets between the common and the river, and he was on a reconnaissance. Years ago as a cub reporter on a provincial paper he had discovered that time spent learning the geography of his area was never wasted. Knowing the lie of the land paid dividends later when quick decisions and quick action were called for, as they might be now. If possible he would avoid doing what Warren called "something drastic" about Jennifer, but one never knew.

He had looked at the house, a neat villa and obviously her parents' home. The walk from the station would take her across the unfrequented common. Would she risk that late at night? Barnes Bridge, the next station down the line, involved a much longer walk, but her route would be through well-lit suburban streets. It would be difficult. He would have to ride on the train with her and see where she got out.

But it was time to meet Angela. He hailed a late-prowling cab and had himself driven over the river to Hammersmith.

She was waiting for him when he got there. He saw her before she saw him. She was the only person he cared about apart from himself and the marvellous thing was that nowadays she really cared for him. Helping him cope with the Lavinia problem had triggered off something in her, she was revelling in the excitement and getting an extra thrill from the need to bottle it all up inside. Watching her hide this inner fever from the world gave him enormous pleasure, he desired her more than ever. Recognising in each other the mad streak of the secret gambler had done wonders for their marriage.

Even when she was badly worried she kept up a front. When she saw him she gave him a fierce smile which made her eyes sparkle. "Hullo. Things are going wrong."

"They do seem to be rather," said Chatham.

"No, but wait till you hear . . ."

Chatham listened intently while she told him exactly what Galbraith had asked her and how she had replied. "The police have got it all worked out, Tony, haven't they?"

"But they can't prove anything. You're a marvel, you handled it amazingly well."

"I was quaking with fright, he was so grim and Presbyterian and Scottish. I felt like Mary Queen of Scots being disapproved of by John Knox."

"Bless you. Were you followed when you left Fontbury to-night?"

"There was a car behind me for a bit, but I dodged about in the lanes and lost it."

"Good, we must be careful from now on, they'll be watching us and we mustn't be caught putting our heads together. I slipped out into Langham Street after the broadcast in case they were watching the front entrance."

"Dear me, things *are* going wrong," said Angela.

"Yes. I think Peter's done something silly and bolted. He was supposed to be taking George Otway down to the cottage, but there's no reply from there."

She looked at him with fresh alarm. "He hasn't got the German pistol, has he?"

"No, Angie. You had it. You were going to put it back in the secret drawer of the bureau. I put it in the glove box of your car for you."

"You said you would, but it wasn't there. I assumed you'd forgotten."

"Damn. Peter must have pinched it back. He hated giving it up."

"Peter with a gun. And Otway. Oh dear, just think of the silly things he might do."

"It is rather worrying. But I briefed him carefully before he met Otway and he was being quite calm and sensible. It may work out right if he keeps his head."

"Then why is there no reply from the cottage?"

"Goodness knows. Could you look in there on your way back to Fontbury and let me know what you find?"

Presently they parted. In the small hours of the morning she rang him from a phone box in Reading. The cottage was all locked up and there was no one there.

Detective-Constable Burton was aggrieved. On the pretext that the Chatham case did not provide enough work for three, Galbraith had had Sergeant Verney taken off it and sent to broaden his horizons by harmless wanderings among the West End vice rings. As a result Burton was run off his feet with a double load of routine leg-work, most of it deadly dull.

And now Galbraith had come back from his excursion to Fontbury in what for him counted as high good humour.

"The woman was lying, Burton, there's nae doubt," he proclaimed. "She's as clever as a basketful of monkeys, but I put the fear of God intae her. They're in it taegether, the three of them, ye can take my word for that."

You bastard, thought Burton, I was the one who spotted that the alibi with the Delage was a stumer. When he first put up the idea Galbraith had told him contemptuously to "cease tae be intoxicated with your own pervairse ingenuity". He had even had the neck to reprimand him formally for poaching on the Berkshire Constabulary's preserves by going to Fontbury himself instead of getting them to check the Chathams' gun room and report. He had also given Verney a rough time for letting him go there, and now the information he had brought back had become Galbraith's own brilliant discovery.

"But tae prove it will be quite another kettle of fish," Galbraith added.

"Yes, Inspector."

"They're losing their nerve, fortunately. Last night Mrs Chatham rushed up tae London tae tell her husband of the fright I'd given her. Leastways, I've nae doubt that'll be where she went, but the Berkshire Constabulary lost track of her in the lanes round Fontbury, through lack of metropolitan sophistication I presume. We can hope for better results from our people here. I have arranged for surveillance on Chatham and Warren as frae this morning."

Burton let him have ten seconds' worth of silent criticism. If Galbraith had been quicker on the uptake he would have had this attended to days ago.

"We've a long way tae go yet tae establish the murder motive," Galbraith mused.

"You're right there, Inspector."

Galbraith sighed. "Spain."

The lugubrious monosyllable made them both shudder. Their painstaking enquiries among the Spanish Republican factions in London had produced only irrelevancies and contradictions, with each informant insisting that all the others were lying. Nothing remotely connected with the case had emerged, apart from charges and counter-charges about Lavinia Mannerton's handling of her mysterious relief money.

"The answer tae our problem must lie in Spain," Galbraith argued. "Lavinia Mannerton was in Spain that winter. She found out something and blackmailed Chatham. What did she find out?"

"Search me, Inspector."

"He stood tae inherit a handsome property and a good income if the nephew died. I tell ye, Burton, it's plainer than a pikestaff. But how are we tae establish that murder was done eleven months ago in a city in foreign parts where whole armies were engaged in massacring each other?"

"I dunno, Inspector," said Burton.

They had put through an enquiry via diplomatic channels, but had little hope of the result.

Galbraith rubbed his rectangular chin. "I've a mind tae question Chatham and give him a rough time. He'll be in a fine state of fright after consulting with his wife."

"I reckon Warren would crack up more easily," said Burton.

"Aye, but we have nae notion how Warren fits intae the conspiracy. Ye believe that Miss Mannerton was blackmailing him as well as Chatham, but about what?"

"Sex," said Burton.

"And why, tell me, would Miss Mannerton be informed of such loose-living habits as Warren may prove tae have?"

Burton made his face completely blank. "I've no idea, Inspector. It was only a guess."

"I've heard she was a bit loose-living herself before she took tae left-wing politics," said Galbraith. Suddenly his eyes were boring into Burton. "Did ye hear any whisper of that when ye were assisting Sergeant Goddard in his enquiries concerning Mrs Meyrick?"

"No, Inspector."

Galbraith went on staring at him hard. Burton returned the stare. He would have come out with everything he knew about Lavinia Mannerton if Galbraith had not been such a bastard.

*

Chatham had eaten no breakfast. When he was as tense as this his stomach was liable to play tricks. He rang the cottage again. There was still no reply and none from Warren's London number.

At half past ten Warren had not shown up at Broadcasting House. His desk diary showed a morning of heavy commitments. He had booked three phone calls to the Far East about arrangements for the Christmas hook-up and at eleven-thirty two Post Office engineers were coming to finalise the circuit bookings. Unless the world-wide circuitry was booked now, the Post Office could not guarantee that lines from Delhi and Fiji and Montreal and Wellington would be available at the right moment on Christmas Day.

Chatham had the long-distance phone bookings transferred to his own extension and began trying to make sense of Warren's notes in time for the meeting with the Post Office. While he was doing this Vine Street police station rang and asked, not very politely, when Inspector Galbraith could come and "question him about some new developments in the case". Chatham said he could come at two. Having spent the wakeful hours of dawn devising answers to almost every question the police could ask, he forced himself not to waste time thinking about the coming interrogation, but concentrated on Warren's circuit diagrams.

Presently he had to pay attention to the new secretary in Warren's office, who was hovering.

"He's written something in his diary for this afternoon," she said, exhibiting it. "The first word looks like 'Christmas' but I'm not very good at reading his writing."

Chatham looked at the entry.

"Perhaps it isn't important, Mr Chatham."

"I'll deal with it," he told her. At three o'clock, Warren had an appointment with King George VI.

He rang higher authority and explained. "If someone high-level could ring the Palace and apologise?"

"That will be attended to. But where is Warren?"

"I'm sorry, I have no idea. I've been worried about him lately, he took Miss Mannerton's death very much to heart. We're still trying to contact him, of course."

"Let me know if you have news. What state is the Christmas hook-up in?"

"I'm looking into that. There seem to be a lot of loose ends. Would you excuse me now, please? We have to book the international circuits today and the Post Office representatives have just arrived."

As usual, the negotiations were laborious, partly because the Post Office believed mistakenly that it spoke the same language as the BBC. In reality it was so entangled in its own regulations that what seemed to the BBC an obvious solution was often rejected by the Post Office as an outrageous violation of all the electrical decencies. As Chatham was trying to prove that what the BBC wanted to fix up with Newfoundland was not unthinkable the telephone rang and Violet began coping in a discreet murmur with what sounded like a troublesome caller. He listened with half an ear.

"Speak up, please, I can't hear you . . . What? Who did you want to speak to? . . . I'm sorry you don't feel well, but this is not a hospital. Yes, this is the BBC, who did you . . . Mr Chatham? I'm sorry, but he's in conference, you can't speak to him now."

Chatham reached for the extension phone. "Who is that? Don't let him ring off."

"Someone very drunk," said Violet.

"Hullo? Chatham here, is that you, Peter?"

But the phone had gone dead.

Helen Thackeray had had a disturbed night. Editorial responsibility did not weigh on her heavily, but responsibility for the BBC's moral reputation did and had kept her awake. When she arrived at Broadcasting House in the morning she knew exactly what she ought to investigate next, but managed to find other tasks which could be classed as urgent. Having dispatched the last of these (a fuss because a speaker had used the word "harlot" at a time when children might be listening) she found herself without an excuse for delay. She knew perfectly well who among her galaxy of well-placed relatives and eminent BBC contacts would be able to tell her the answer, but for a moment the name eluded her. Having recognised the lapse of memory as Freudian, she rang the Foreign

Office, asked for a limp young sprig of the nobility in the Personnel Department called, as she now remembered, Lord Ampleforth, reminded him that they had met over lunch at his mother's, and asked him to do her a favour.

"Oh, er, yes?" bleated Lord Ampleforth, who remembered the lunch vividly. The formidable BBC lady had terrified him out of his wits.

"I'm trying to find out who was *en poste* at Madrid in December last year."

"Oh, but I think the Embassy had withdrawn to Hendaye by then, for safety, you know."

"Quite. But didn't they keep on someone minor like a second secretary in Madrid to look after distressed British subjects and so on?"

"Oh goodness yes, I remember now. Hold on while I look at the list . . . It seems to have been a Mr J. K. Wilbraham, but I'm afraid I don't know him."

"Where is he now?" Helen interrupted.

"Let's see . . . oh dear, Helsinki. Terribly boring, poor man."

Helen thanked him and saw with relief that it was almost lunch time. The whole afternoon would be taken up with a meeting. By the time it broke up it would be too late to ring Helsinki. That would have to wait till tomorrow.

Her meeting was about the new-fangled grading system, an organised promotion structure which was to be substituted for the chaotic but inspired personal judgments of Sir John Reith. Helen, who hated the way the BBC had transformed itself from an adventure to an institution, was bored to stupefaction. Suddenly she found herself thinking about her cousin Margaret, who nursed wounded soldiers throughout the war. The duty Margaret had dreaded most was in the ward for self-inflicted wounds, full of pathetic men who had shot themselves, usually in the foot, to escape from the horror of the trenches. One had to treat them as criminals while one dressed their wounds . . .

My brain must be rotting, Helen told herself. Why on earth should I think of that now?

*

Chatham had not met Inspector Galbraith before, but recognised him at once from Angela's description. Burton was with him, and settled down at Violet's empty desk with his notebook as the grim-mouthed Galbraith uttered the routine warning that anything Chatham said would be "taken down in writing and might be used in evidence".

"Now, Mr Chatham. Nae doubt your wife has informed ye about the enquiries I made yesterday at Fontbury Manor."

"I'm sorry, no. My wife is about to divorce me, we don't communicate often."

"Then ye would deny that ye had a clandestine meeting with her last night tae discuss the matter?"

A guess, Chatham decided. He and Angela had made quite sure they were not being followed.

"Inspector, I'm afraid you haven't grasped the situation. Mrs Chatham would only agree to meet me in the presence of her lawyers."

"Last night she gave the slip tae police officers who were keeping her under observation. Why would she do that now?"

"I imagine she thought they were private detectives hired by me to find out who she was spending the night with. But I'm only guessing, you must ask her."

Galbraith blinked and changed the subject. "On the afternoon of Miss Mannerton's death the indoor servants, all but one, were away out of the house. Ye had no knowledge of this, I presume?"

Chatham sidestepped the trap easily. "I knew about Harrison, that's the butler, having a row with her and being ordered out of the house, if that's what you mean. Harrison rang me and asked what he should do."

"And ye told him tae spend the night at his sister's in Reading."

"Yes. My wife was obviously in a wildly excited state. I thought it would be better."

Galbraith drew himself up to his full height. His mouth opened and shut rigidly, like the lower jaw of a ventriloquist's dummy. "Mr Chatham, I suggest that ye are lying. I have reason tae believe that ye did not visit your wife at Fontbury Manor on the day in question. I believe that instead of proceeding tae Fontbury ye concealed yourself in room four hundred and fifty-seven at the Langham Hotel, London, and shot Miss Mannerton."

Chatham was silent, wondering what aces Galbraith had up his sleeve.

"Have ye no answer tae this accusation?" Galbraith thundered.

"I'm sorry, I was too bewildered. I can only say that without wishing to be offensive I can't imagine what 'reason' you could have for believing anything so absurd."

He waited, very afraid, for Galbraith to produce his aces. But seemingly there were none. Galbraith blinked, and changed the subject.

"Ye have a very distinctive car, Mr Chatham. A big Delage."

"Yes." He blinks when he's at a loss, Chatham told himself, or when he loses a trick he expected to win.

"Have ye lent it on any occasion tae Mr Peter Warren?"

"Yes. He has it at the moment, in fact. I lent it to him last night."

Had they found the Delage abandoned somewhere? Or had they even arrested and questioned Warren? If so, what had he said?

"But why," Galbraith asked, "would ye be lending a valuable car tae a man ye are on very bad terms with?"

"Because I hope he'll take a fancy to it and buy it from me, I'm tired of driving anything so big."

Galbraith blinked. Or rather it was a cross between a blink and a twitch.

"Did ye not lend it tae him on the day of the fatality?"

"No, I was using it. As you know, I drove down to Fontbury to try to calm my wife."

"Taking three hours for a journey which normally takes two."

"Does it? There are those road works on the A4 in Reading, it takes quite a time to get through."

"I put it tae ye, Chatham, Warren was driving the car and the delay was due tae the time he had tae spend at Royal Lodge."

"My dear Galbraith, think for a moment. Do you seriously suggest that he drove up to Royal Lodge under the noses of the guards and so on, in a car which he planned to use later in the afternoon to establish a false alibi for me?"

Galbraith blinked twice. No doubt he had guessed: Peter had

switched temporarily from the Delage to his own Chrysler somewhere in Windsor Great Park, but how could the police prove it?

"May I ask a question?" Chatham went on. "I'm worried about Peter Warren. He didn't turn up for work this morning and his landlady says he didn't come home last night. D'you know where he is?"

Galbraith produced a different kind of blink. Astonishment.

"I was about tae put the same question tae you, Mr Chatham. My men have been trying to trace him all day."

"Oh? I hope they find him," said Chatham, managing somehow not to show his relief. "I'd like to know what's happened to my car."

Galbraith gave him a disbelieving stare. Perhaps he suspected him of spiriting the nerve-wracked Warren away out of reach of police questioning.

Chatham decided that the moment had come to go over to the attack. "Could we discuss my motive now, Inspector? If you're accusing me of murdering Miss Mannerton no doubt you think I killed her for some reason."

"We willna discuss that at this stage, my enquiries are not complete."

"Couldn't I help you complete them? I'll try if you tell me what you suspect."

Galbraith blinked but said nothing.

"Aren't you being a little unpractical, Inspector? Why creep around London detecting when I've said I'll tell you anything you want to know?"

"It is in Madrid, not London, that I am causing enquiries tae be made."

"In Madrid?" Chatham echoed in well-bred surprise. "Surely you haven't fallen for that newspaper nonsense about me and the Spanish Reds?"

"I have not, Mr Chatham, and your parade of bewildered innocence doesna deceive me. Ye know very well what I have in mind."

"No really, I assure you."

"On the death of your nephew Michael," Galbraith thundered,

"ye succeeded tac a handsome property and a very substantial income."

"But . . . dear me, what has my inheriting Fontbury to do with shooting Miss Mannerton? Unless . . . oh, I see! You think I killed Michael as well." His smile was not forced this time. He was beginning to enjoy himself.

"It is intae the manner of your nephew's death that I have caused enquiries tae be made in Madrid."

"But my dear fellow, why didn't you tell me earlier? I could have saved you so much trouble." He wrote rapidly on a memo pad. "Here's the address of our family solicitor, get him to show you Michael's death certificate. It's dated 27th November last year. I didn't leave here till December 1st to go to Madrid, I had a broadcast the night before. There's probably a Spanish entry stamp in my passport dated the second, I'll look. Why didn't you come out with this at once instead of beating about the bush till I dragged it out of you? Then we wouldn't have wasted so much of each other's time."

SIXTEEN

PETER WARREN LIT a cigarette, belched, and went on concentrating on the only task he felt equal to now: shutting out from his mind the knowledge of the fix he was in.

Last night his first reaction had been to put all the distance he could between himself and Regent's Park. From habit he had made for the A4. As he reached open country he realised that what he longed for was that never failing opiate, a woman.

He found what he wanted in Slough. It comforted him for a time. But in the small hours he was roughly woken from a heavy sleep, to find himself being haggled with over money in a sordid room by an unappetising whore who took all his cash off him and turned him out into the cold dawn. As he sat in the Delage wondering what to do next, he remembered: there was an almost full bottle of whisky at the Marlow cottage.

Now, six hours later, the bottle was empty and he had started on the gin. The telephone had rung some time during the morning but he had a blinding headache and felt too ill to answer it. It occurred to him that he had an appointment with the King at three. He giggled at the thought of himself reeling and retching while the monarch stuttered in pop-eyed astonishment at his antics. He had tried to ring Chatham and arrange for an apology to be sent, but that bitch Violet had mucked everything up as usual so to hell with it. He decided not to bother and slept for a time. When he woke it was late afternoon and he was cold.

"Excuse me, Madam," said Harrison. "There is a person on the telephone who has rung twice and insists on speaking to you. But I am sorry to say that he is very drunk."

She went to the phone. ". . . Angie?" said a faint voice at the other end.

"Peter. Where are you?"

"Bloody awful."

"I daresay, but where?"

"Angie, I'm so miserable. I'm all by myself and it's getting dark."

"Listen, Peter. Where are you?"

". . . Cottage . . ."

"Are you alone or is someone else there?"

"Wha? . . ."

"Is Otway there with you?"

"No!" Alarmingly, he began to sob. "Angie, for God's sake, come. Bring some drink."

"Very well, Peter. I'll be with you as soon as I can."

After thinking for several minutes, Angela made preparations for departure which were brief but curious. She sought out a locked suitcase in the attic and transferred the contents to a shopping basket. Thus equipped, she drove out of the great gates in her two-seater and made for the A4 and Reading.

As she passed the pub at the bottom of the village street a car with two men in it pulled out and took up station fifty yards behind her. It had been waiting in the pub forecourt since the morning, no doubt causing much comment in the village. Its occupants could only be plain-clothes policemen.

"Keep close up, Ron," said one of them. "Don't lose her, like Fred and Dick did last night."

Their instructions were that it did not matter if Mrs Chatham spotted them. On the contrary, it would do no harm to give her a good fright.

Angela drove into the centre of Reading and parked. The police car parked nearby. Followed by the policemen she dawdled in and out of a shop or two, then plunged into a crowded department store.

"She's trying to shake us off, Ron. You cover the other entrance."

"There's three, sarge."

"Damn. Can you see her anywhere?"

"No . . . Yes, there she is, going upstairs."

They followed. But there was no sign of Mrs Chatham when they reached the upper floor. By the time they had worked out that she must be in the Ladies Rest Room, she was halfway downstairs, having exchanged what she was wearing for the contents of her shopping basket. The receptionist at the Langham Hotel might have recognised the grey-haired country lady in the ill-fitting tweed suit, but the Berkshire Constabulary walked straight past her without a glance. Presently it occurred to them to go and see if her car was still there. By then she was well on her way to the cottage.

It was quite dark when she reached it. No light showed from the windows but the Delage was parked behind it and the back door was unlocked. A sound of heavy snoring came from the living room. She drew the curtains and turned on the light.

Peter Warren was lying on the sofa face downwards, with an empty gin bottle and a glass on the carpet beside him. She turned him over and shook him.

"Wake up. It's me. Angie."

"Wha? . . . Oh. Hullo, Angie."

"What's happened? Where's George Otway?"

He gazed at her stupidly.

"Where's the gun?"

"What gun? . . ."

The German pistol was nowhere in the room and she could get no sense out of him. Seizing a torch she went out to search the Delage, and found it under the driver's seat. The magazine was empty. She thought for a moment, then transferred it to the glove pocket of her own car.

"Peter. You shot him, didn't you? Tell me. Wake up and talk sense."

". . . Don't want to talk about it . . . Want a drink."

She shook him. "Where is he? Come on, tell me."

". . . Drink."

"I shan't get you one till you tell me. Where is he?"

"In the bushes. Regent's Park. Dead."

"Why? What happened?"

"Shut up, Angie, I don't want to think about it. Go away."

He turned over again on to his face. She could get no more out of him. Presently he began to snore. What would Tony have done, Angela wondered. He would have done nothing until he had looked carefully at all the possible courses of action, like a chess player. He would calculate how his opponent would respond to each of the possible moves and how things would develop after that . . . suddenly it was quite clear what Tony would do in her place, and rather exciting to take on herself the responsibility for doing it.

Warren was still heavily asleep. She tiptoed into the bathroom and opened the medicine cabinet. The first aid things were still there and she helped herself to what she needed. Then she went back to Warren and shook him awake. "Here, I've brought you these."

He squinted up at her blearily. "I don't want any bloody aspirin."

"Yes, you do, Peter," she shouted. "You want the lot. The whole bottleful."

There was a stunned moment while he took this in. Then he started to sob. "No, Angie, no, please. I couldn't, I'm afraid. Why won't you get me a drink?"

"Drink won't do you one bit of good, Peter. When you sober up you'll still be afraid. Don't you want to stop being afraid?"

"Oh yes, Angie, but—"

"Listen. You've killed Otway and the police know why you did it. They'll come here and find you and you'll be hanged for murder, why go through all that? It's only prolonging the agony."

"Where's Tony? Tony will get me out of this, he'll tell me what to do. Where is he, I must ask him."

Angela squared her shoulders and stared him sternly in the face. "I have asked him," she lied, and held the aspirin bottle inches before his eyes. "This is what he told me."

"No. No, he'd never say that. He's my best friend."

"He was. He isn't anymore. He's disappointed in you, Peter, you let him down. Even before you shot Otway he was saying he'd never forgive you, never speak to you again."

"He didn't say that," cried Warren between sobs. "He can't have, you're lying."

"Nonsense. I've brought you some water. Here you are, take half a dozen for a start."

"He didn't say that, Angie. Tell me he didn't."

"Here. Take these and stop wasting time."

"Oh my God . . . Why have you got your gloves on, Angie?"

"Why the hell d'you think? No, don't mess about, the police'll be here soon and they'll pump you out so that you can be hanged for murder which won't be any more enjoyable. Go on, put them all in. Here's the water, now swallow. Well done, here are six more . . . Of course you can swallow them, don't be such a baby . . . No, damn you, twelve isn't enough, you're going to take the whole bottleful, here are some more. Well done . . . No! No, Peter, don't you dare vomit, I forbid you to vomit, you're going to keep the whole lot down if I have to hold your mouth shut. Have a bit of a rest now, then you'll feel better. Just think of it, no more feeling afraid, no more wondering if you'll be caught . . . Can you manage the rest now? Come on, you might as well . . . Oh, well done. This is by far the best way, now you can lie back and relax."

After a little while he said, "Angie, are you still there?"

"Yes, Peter."

"You see, Angie, he was the only real friend I had."

Presently he began drifting into unconsciousness. Angela turned off the lights and sat beside him in the dark listening to the change in his breathing. Now that the battle of wills was over she was trembling violently and had to fight down nausea. Had Tony felt like that after he had shot Lavinia? She must ask him as soon as it was safe for them to talk.

She admired Tony enormously for what he had done and for the steely nerve he had shown when the going got rough. He had done it mostly for her, of course. He had come to terms long ago with being the younger brother and the uncle of the next heir. Unlike her he had no hankerings after landed gentry status, what mattered to him was the climb to top dog status in the BBC. But he knew what Fontbury meant to her, that was why he had taken the risk in the first place; and when he had to, in the second and third.

As she sat there waiting for Peter to die she was sure Tony would be pleased with her.

Presently the telephone rang. She stared at it in horror, then lifted the receiver and waited, without speaking.

She heard Chatham's voice.

"Is that you, Peter?" he asked.

"No, it's me."

"Is Peter there?"

"Yes."

"What's happening?"

"I hesitate to tell you."

"It's all right. I'm in a phone box at the club."

"Peter's been drinking heavily and now he's taken an overdose."

"Fatal?"

"Yes."

"And—George?"

"I understand that that was also fatal."

"Oh, nonsense."

"That's what Peter told me. He was very fuddled, of course."

Suddenly Chatham began to laugh.

"What's so funny?" asked Angela nervily.

"Half an hour ago I saw the alleged corpse walking out of Broadcasting House with a girl on his arm."

When Angela had recovered from the shock she began to laugh too.

Now, twenty-four hours later, George Otway had calmed down after having the fright of his life. It began when he slammed the driver's door of the Delage on Warren and his pistol. As a tactic for covering his escape this was ineffective. Warren's foot was already out of the car so that the door would not shut. Before he had run ten yards Warren was out in the road, hopping with pain on one foot and firing the gun wildly. The only cover available was one of the dismal little shrubberies surrounding the park. It was guarded by spiky iron railings, but fear gave George the strength to vault them and he crashed down noisily among privet and laurel bushes. Pursued by bullets he fought his way deeper into the shrubbery, but it soon dawned on him that Warren was aiming at the noise he was making. For half a minute he stood still, then crouched and began to move again cautiously. But the shrubbery was thickly planted and despite precautions twigs cracked. A bullet came uncomfortably close. As he flung himself down a low branch poked him sharply in the eye. He gave a shout of rage and pain, quickly checked in case Warren used it to aim on. There was a very long silence.

"George?" Warren called in a muted, panic-stricken voice. "I say, you're not dead, are you?"

Silence. Warren, fat, drink-sodden and out of condition, was in no state to vault over four-foot iron railings with spikes on top. His panic-stricken footsteps ran up and down as he tried to find an easier way into the shrubbery, but all the entrances to the park from the Outer Circle were locked for the night. He came back to the point where George had climbed over and called again. "George?"

George lay still and waited. A passing car swept by and for a moment its headlights picked him out.

"Oh my God," Warren moaned.

The Delage's engine started and it moved away.

Strength inspired by fear had got George over the railings on the way into the shrubbery. Strength fuelled by anger got him' out again. His first thought was to go straight to the police, and he walked fast towards Albany Street. The police, then perhaps the newspapers. Warren ought to be shown up.

But as he reached Chester Gate he slowed down. The story would be incomplete unless he talked about the deeply shaming fate which had overtaken Annie. Did he really intend to let that be plastered all over the newspapers? If that happened, his family would never speak to him again.

These were sound reasons for hesitating, but there was a more decisive argument for keeping quiet. He did not think of it as blackmail. It was more what businessmen called compensation for loss of office. Warren had better think again if he expected to get away with a measly four pounds a week.

No, he would not go to the police. And there were even stronger motives for keeping quiet about his adventure when he met

Jennifer next evening. A sordid, shameful story which began with an abortion was quite unfit for the ears of a young lady.

Chatham stood on Waterloo station. He had pretended to be waiting for a speaker in the hall at Broadcasting House and watched, powerless to intervene, as George Otway arrived to keep his date with Jennifer. They had gone to see the Ziegfield Follies of 1937, which finished at ten according to the timetable outside the cinema. It was now ten-thirty. Unless they lingered for a chat and drink Jennifer should arrive at any moment to catch her train to Barnes. Otway had almost certainly given her a lurid account of whatever had happened between him and Warren. The moment was approaching when "something drastic" would have to be done.

He had taken elaborate precautions, changing platforms on the underground and so on, and thought he had shaken off any pursuit. But a young policeman in a sports jacket and grey flannels, one of a team of four shadowers, had just followed his example and bought a ticket to Barnes Bridge and was wondering who he was waiting to meet at the barrier. Trains on the Barnes-Richmond line had come and gone. Whoever it was seemed to be late.

At ten-forty Jennifer Howe stormed up the steps from the Underground in a very bad temper. Her evening with George Otway had been a disaster of embarrassment and boredom. He had pretended unconvincingly to be eager to spend far more on her than he could possibly afford, then treated her to tepid baked beans on soggy toast in an alarmingly sordid cafe. During this repulsive meal he had talked solidly about football, and when she tried to change the subject by taking an interest in his job problem with the BBC he had gone bright red and clammed up on her. Later he assumed that his very modest expenditure entitled him to put his arm round her while they watched a tasteless and inane film. Moreover his hair oil smelt.

As she hurried towards the Richmond-Barnes platform she caught sight of a familiar figure. Chatham. He had seen her and was coming towards her smiling. She had had her bellyful of one unwanted admirer. Must she now cope with another? How dare he, at this time of night? For this was no chance meeting. She had caught him eyeing her covertly while she waited for Otway in the hall at Broadcasting House and was not deceived for a moment by his elaborate explanation of why he was going to Barnes, something about his wife being in the flat and turning him out to sleep with friends there for some technical reason connected with the divorce. As he explained all this he hurried along beside her, then opened the door of an empty compartment and waited for her to get in.

No, she decided. He was obviously a sex maniac and would probably try to rape her in the train. "Mr Chatham, d'you mind if I travel by myself? I'm very tired and I wouldn't be good company."

"Oh nonsense, my dear, you can't walk across Barnes Common by yourself at this time of night, I'll walk you home."

"Thank you, but I don't think I can stand any more male company, I've just had a very tiresome evening with a young man who talked about nothing but football. Goodnight."

Carriage doors were slamming. The whistle blew.

"You're making me miss my train," she snapped. But Chatham stood still, blocking the carriage door.

"Was that all George Otway talked about?"

She slapped his face hard, then dodged past him into the train. "Yes. He was an even worse bore than you are."

The train moved off. Chatham stood on the platform rubbing his face. Serve him right, thought the young policeman in grey flannels, no wonder his wife's divorcing him.

Chatham's thoughts were different. For the first time for days, he was pretty sure he would get away with murder.

SEVENTEEN

"I'M NOT SURE, Mr Wilbraham," said Helen Thackeray on the line to Helsinki, "what use the BBC will be able to make of all this material I'm collecting. But I'm sure we ought to do something about all these young poets who are fighting for their ideals in Spain."

"I doubt if I can help you," said the distant voice nervously.

"I'm stuck for the biographical details of some of them, Michael Chatham, for instance. Someone told me he'd been shot for spying for the fascists. I hope that's not true?"

Mr Wilbraham lapsed into thoughtful silence.

"Oh dear," said Helen. "You obviously know about this. I really must get the story straight in case I involve the BBC in controversy."

Mr Wilbraham decided that in the circumstances he would have to overcome his distrust of journalists. "Since you know so much," he said, "perhaps it will be best if I tell you the facts."

He did so in great detail: the young man on the embassy doorstep with an envelope, the scuffle with the two secret policemen who pounced as he handed the envelope to the doorman, the doorman's refusal to give it up, Michael's inability to explain or even understand what the trouble was, because he spoke no Spanish.

"You see, Miss Thackeray, Madrid was full of spy scares at the time because some genuine fascist spies had just been caught. The authorities were very tense and nervous and embassies like ours which maintained a, shall we say, neutral posture came in for a lot of suspicion. So the police dragged the poor young man away and shot him against the wall of the corner shop."

"How dreadful . . . And what was in the envelope?"

"Nothing compromising, I assure you. He'd made a will and

decided to hand it to us for safe keeping. It was a sad business really. The young man wouldn't have been mistaken for a spy if he hadn't had the idea of leaving his few possessions to some relative or sweetheart at home."

"Dear me. I wonder who the beneficiary was."

"I've no idea, I handed the envelope unopened to the next of kin, an uncle I think, who came out to Madrid to enquire. But—wait! I think he said he worked for the BBC. Does the name 'Chatham' mean anything to you?"

"Yes, I think it does," Helen managed.

"He could probably give you more information than I can. And there was someone else, an Englishwoman who worked in one of the Madrid hospitals. She was a friend of the young man's and came to enquire. But that was some weeks later."

"Do you remember her name?"

"I'm sorry, no. But if you want to contact her, perhaps Mr Chatham could help."

When the phone call was over Helen Thackeray took a taxi to Somerset House, with her mind in a turmoil. What she found in the records there forced her to conclude that what Michael Chatham's last will and testament contained was anyone's guess. The will presented for probate had been executed a month before he left England, and was obviously the work of the Chatham family solicitor. As he had died unmarried and without issue, its effect was to leave "everything of which I die possessed to my said uncle, Anthony Harold de Courcy Chatham".

"Inspector Galbraith? Tony Chatham here, good morning. Have you found any trace of Peter Warren yet?"

"We have not, and the matter begins tae assume a sinister aspect."

"Yes, it's very worrying. I've just remembered something that might help. There's a country cottage he borrows quite often. The owner's abroad. You might find some clue there."

"Have ye the address?"

"No, but it's somewhere near Marlow, I think. He left us the phone number in case of emergency, could you trace it from that?"

"Aye, Mr Chatham. Give me the number and I'll see tae the matter."

"He shot at me, Mr Chatham," said George Otway. "He tried to kill me."

"Really? It sounds very unlike him, unless you'd been threatening him at all. I think he mentioned a previous occasion when you made a very savage and brutal attack on him, and he may have been afraid that you'd do it again."

George shifted uncomfortably in his chair.

"He wasn't himself, you know," Chatham went on. "He was very distressed about his secretary's death."

"He'd no call to shoot at me because of that."

"Of course not, but he probably thought he was acting in self-defence. After all, you were threatening him. The police call it 'demanding money with menaces'."

"I wanted him to get back my job, that he lost for me."

"Oh dear, he could never understand why you accused him of that. I'm wondering, you see, what sort of impression it would make if you turned up at the inquest and told this story. It would look, don't you think, as if a man who was already in great distress of mind was pushed over the edge into suicide by the threats of a blackmailer. That wouldn't improve your job prospects, would it?"

"What job prospects have I got?" George blurted out. "If I give the BBC as a reference they'll say I was sacked for being drunk on duty."

Suddenly Chatham was smiling at him. It made him feel he had found a friend.

"You know, George, I think I might be able to get you over that. What sort of job had you in mind?"

"I'd like the RAF. What with this war coming they're looking for radio technicians."

"What a very good idea. When you apply give the recruiting officer my name. I'll give you a personal reference and make sure the official BBC one isn't too bad. But on one condition: Peter Warren was a friend of mine, I won't have wrong done to his memory. From now on, some unknown person doctored your beer as a practical joke that went wrong. Agreed?"

The coroner looked over the top of his glasses at Chatham. Galbraith had run out of excuses for postponement and the inquest on Peter Warren was under way at last.

"You say he was under great nervous strain, Mr Chatham. Why?"

"He had heavy responsibilities as my deputy. On top of that, he was looking after the big Christmas Day programme, which involved a lot of complicated negotiations with overseas broadcasting organisations and so on. But most of all, I think, he was deeply distressed by the death of his secretary, Miss Mannerton. He felt, quite wrongly, that he was partly responsible for it."

"Why should he have felt that?"

"On the day before his suicide he confessed to me something that he had denied up to then to the police. It was he who had made a phone call to Miss Mannerton asking her to go into my office and find a piece of information that he needed. By a very unfortunate coincidence she did so at the moment when that madman or whoever he was was waiting in the hotel room opposite to shoot me."

"Hm. Why did he deny making the call in the first place?"

"At the time of her death he was very distressed and I think lost his head. Afterwards he thought he'd look guilty if he changed his story."

"Guilty? Why did he think he'd look guilty?"

"There was a police theory at one time, I believe, that Miss Mannerton was the intended murder victim, and that the threatening letters and attacks on me were a blind."

While the coroner puzzled this out with Chatham's help, Inspector Galbraith ground his teeth with rage. Chatham was lying. But nothing could be proved. The only fingerprints on the aspirin bottle were Warren's, indeed the only fingerprints in the cottage were his. Chatham and his wife had covered their tracks completely, and now they even had the nerve to bring back into existence the mythical Irish assassin in whom nobody seriously believed.

When Chatham first told him the fairy story about Warren's "confession" Galbraith spotted the weakness in it at once.

"I have tae admire your ingenuity, Mr Chatham. But ye've overlooked something. There were two phone calls."

"Were there? Peter only mentioned one to me."

"There was the one Warren made from the call box in Oxford and the one ye made yourself from the Langham Hotel."

"I don't want to sound impatient, Galbraith, but do try to get this absurd idea out of your mind. How could I have been in the Langham Hotel and at the same time in Berkshire having a heated argument with my wife?"

"I'll ask the questions, please. How do ye account for the two phone calls?"

"If I may say so, my dear Galbraith, accounting for things is your job, not mine. I've repeated to you what Peter Warren told me, and there my responsibility ends."

The weakness in the story was not a weakness after all, when Galbraith came to think of it. The duplicate phone calls strongly suggested that Warren, far from being the innocent cause of Lavinia Mannerton's death, was an accomplice in a plot to kill her. But weeks of hard detective work had failed to unearth any scrap of proof that he was an accomplice of Chatham's. Galbraith tried to imagine himself going to the Director of Public Prosecutions and expounding the elaborate, unproven theory which he knew to be the truth. He would be the laughing stock of Scotland Yard. The coroner and the public might as well be left to believe that Lavinia Mannerton had been shot by a madman who intended to kill Chatham.

Helen Thackeray sat in court watching Chatham give evidence. She had spent long nights staring sleeplessly at the ceiling and trying to decide where her duty lay. Chatham was a murderer, without knowing the mechanics of what he had done she was sure of that, and murderers should not be left at large. On the other hand he had murdered a woman who had blackmailed him and goodness knew how many of his colleagues. If she went to the police with what she knew skeletons would come tumbling out of the BBC cupboard by the dozen.

It would be criminal to drag the Corporation through the mud. Very soon—next year perhaps—there would be a European War. When it came, the country would need the BBC, its reputation for decency and steadiness and trustworthy information was a national asset which must not be squandered. This was no time to expose its feet of clay.

Chatham had killed once and might kill again. Did that matter, when butchery on a mass scale would begin in a matter of months? Perhaps not. But at the next programme board, when he tried to sit next to her, she quickly motioned someone else into the vacant chair.

"Well, Angie, that's that," said Chatham.

Angela looked up from the chest of drawers she was ransacking. "Yes, thank goodness."

She had come up to Imperial Mansions to collect clothes for a Mediterranean cruise. They would miss each other badly but there had to be a decent interval of estrangement before they took up life together again. An abrupt reconciliation would confirm Galbraith in his suspicions and bewilder Gerald yet further.

"Were you very frightened?" Chatham asked. "I was."

"Yes. We kept our heads and we got away with it, but only because we had amazing luck. If we're ever tempted again we must keep saying 'we were damn lucky, don't let's risk it, we might not be lucky again'."

"Will you miss the excitement?" Chatham asked.

"Yes, but next time I shall take up something legal like parachute jumping."

"When we started I didn't foresee that we'd have to be as illegal as this. One thing led to another, all because Michael made that idiotic will."

But one couldn't blame Michael really. He was almost a boy still and he was expecting to die. Letters from England were not getting through and he had no idea when he made the will that his grandfather had collapsed and died suddenly from a totally unexpected heart attack. The girl had "befriended" him as he put it, on one of his brief respites from the front and he had intended to leave her a few hundred pounds in Post Office Savings Certificates and the balance of his Oxford bank account. What he had done was to leave Fontbury to an illiterate peasant girl from a village outside Madrid who made little attempt when Chatham went to see her to hide the fact that she was the village whore.

To destroy the will was merely to make sure that Michael's real intentions were carried out. On thinking it over carefully Chatham decided it was quite safe. The Thaelmann Battalion was well on the way to becoming a heroic legend by dint of being wiped out. The two members of the British contingent who had witnessed the will were already dead. Any survivor who knew about it would think its terms were being complied with, because he had arranged to give the girl roughly what Michael thought he was leaving her, a thousand pounds at most.

It all seemed perfectly safe. But he had reckoned without Lavinia Mannerton.

In a year or eighteen months there would be a war, he decided. The BBC would have a key role to play, a post at the top would be interesting. But Helen Thackeray seemed to have gone off him, there were moments when he wondered if she suspected something. Without her support he might not be able to push up through the dead wood to the top in time, and even if he did, would it satisfy him? The real action would be elsewhere, and Angela would despise him if he sat in Broadcasting House juggling with words instead of getting his teeth into some deeds. He would put out feelers in Whitehall. If he wanted the power to shape events and manage people he must find the right opening soon. Some undercover intelligence thing would be just right for him . . .

When Jennifer Howe's first novel was accepted by a publisher she left the BBC and wrote another, which was very well reviewed and ran into a second edition. The BBC then decided that she was no longer beneath its notice and enlisted her as a talks producer. After the war she married her head of department and produced three children and a steady stream of middlebrow fiction.

George Otway married his cousin and was shot down over the Ruhr in a Lancaster in 1941. Helen Thackeray became a temporary civil servant on the outbreak of war, and ended it as a very senior permanent one. Chatham, whose war consisted of high-powered intrigue in Cairo, launched into politics in the first post-war election and she followed his career with interest. He soon reached ministerial rank. But she was not surprised when he came a cropper in one of the big corruption scandals of the sixties. People who get away with it once never really believe that they won't be lucky again.